How could she ex

Turning abruptly, he knocked her purse off the counter and stooped to pick up the scattered items.

"Don't worry about that," she said hastily, rushing to kneel beside him. "I'll take care of it." She reached for the folded piece of paper that he held in his hand.

Daniel met her gaze and held it for a long moment. Then, shifting his eyes to the paper, he unfolded it. The silence between them became electric with tension as he slowly read the words printed there.

When he raised his eyes to the woman beside him, they both stood, staring at each other warily.

"It seems there was something you forgot to tell me," he said softly, glancing again at what appeared to be his own marriage license.

Dear Reader,

Spellbinders! That's what we're striving for. The editors at Silhouette are determined to capture your imagination and win your heart with every single book we publish. Each month, six Special Editions are chosen with *you* in mind.

Our authors are our inspiration. Writers such as Nora Roberts, Tracy Sinclair, Kathleen Eagle, Carole Halston and Linda Howard—to name but a few—are masters at creating endearing characters and heartrending love stories. Their characters are everyday people—just like you and me—whose lives have been touched by love, whose dream and desire suddenly comes true!

So find a cozy, quiet place to read, and create your own special moment with a Silhouette Special Edition.

Sincerely,

Rosalind Noonan
Senior Editor
SILHOUETTE BOOKS

BILLIE GREEN
A Special Man

Silhouette Special Edition

Published by Silhouette Books New York

America's Publisher of Contemporary Romance

To Mikie, a sane Alice brought by some misplaced
miracle to our Wonderland, for which we all
constantly thank God . . . and Mama and Daddy's
lack of abstinence.

 SILHOUETTE BOOKS
300 East 42nd St., New York, N.Y. 10017

ISBN: 0-373-09346-2

First Silhouette Books printing November 1986

Books by Billie Green

Silhouette Special Edition

Jesse's Girl #297
A Special Man #346

BILLIE GREEN's

college professor once told her that she was a *natural* writer. But her readers and editors find it hard to believe that she writes one good story after another only because she comes by them naturally. Maybe someday this devoted wife, mother of three and romance writer extraordinaire will create a heroine who is a writer. Then, possibly, we will get a hint of her trials and tribulations.

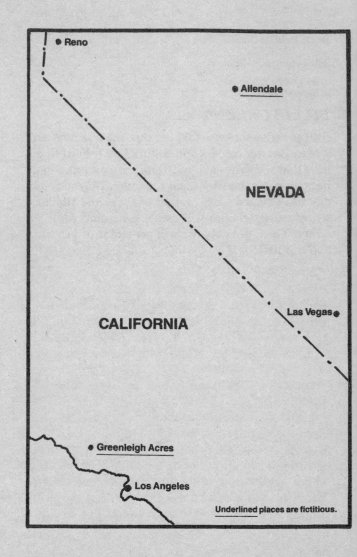

Underlined places are fictitious.

Chapter One

If it were an English night, and if she were given to melancholic freaks, Amanda might have compared the drive that lay before her to the second Mrs. de Winter's tormented dream of a return to Manderley.

But it was Southern California and Amanda was not in the least bit melancholic. Today the closest she had come to that state of mind was when the guard at the iron gate behind her had immediately accepted that she and the anemic creature pictured on her driver's license were one and the same.

Gravel crunched beneath the tires as she followed the twisting and turning of the drive. The woods on either side were artfully natural. No tortured trees here, she thought with a smile. No long, tenacious fingers of nature plucked at the road. The fingers of nature in California had more of a tendency to wave gaily, she thought, laughing softly as the warm breeze ruffled her long, brown hair.

But even with the lovely scenery, anticipation made the drive seem interminable. With each turn of the road, her fingers gripped the steering wheel a little tighter.

Just when she had decided she had somehow gained entry to a state park and would at any moment be surrounded by fervent picnickers, she broke out of the woods, and Greenleigh Acres stood before her.

The beauty of the house took her breath away. Here in Santa Barbara County was an English country home, ivy-covered walls and all. It sat peacefully in an open pocket of land. From the huge central block, symmetrical wings extended, bending slightly inward like arms guarding the driveway and front garden. Lush green lawn surrounded all, ending only at the cliff that overlooked the blue waters of the Pacific. It was extravagantly serene. No devil rode here, Amanda thought, her eyes wide as she stared in open pleasure.

The gravel road looped, becoming a circular drive that enclosed a formal garden, the kind that always reminded Amanda of the Queen of Hearts's croquet grounds. In the center, a fountain splashed water into marble shells, liquid silver glittering in the sun.

Did one knock at the door of a resort? Amanda wondered seconds later as she took the first of the wide steps before her. It seemed impertinent somehow just to walk into what looked like a private home.

One of the massive doors opened as she gained the top step, solving her dilemma. A couple in casual clothes bounced down the steps, talking and laughing. Each had that special look that only people with a moneyed background could achieve.

Glancing down at her neat linen suit—her best—Amanda shrugged and stepped inside to a vast, high-ceilinged room. Clusters of furniture—antique from the look of it—were arranged around the room. Each grouping had a curiously intimate appearance, giving the feel of privacy to the guests who sat and talked in hushed tones while others passed through in riding habits or swimwear.

Amanda smiled. She felt curiously invisible and was almost tempted to stand on a chair and shout, "I'm Princess Di in disguise, and you all just screwed up royally." But she needed this job, and instead she glanced around, searching for anyone who resembled an employee.

To one side of the room, a plump woman, her ash-brown hair dulled by a vivid white tennis dress, stood speaking to an elderly woman. The harried expression on her face, more than the clipboard in her hand, indicated a woman who worked for her living.

"No, Mrs. Hadley," the plump woman was saying as Amanda approached. "Helga didn't forget you. You're scheduled for a massage at eleven o'clock. Not ten."

"I always have my massage at ten o'clock, young woman. Always." The word was punctuated by a jabbing finger to the younger woman's shoulder. "Mrs. Oates will hear about this. Don't think she won't. You've obviously allowed someone to buy my time with the masseuse. This time your greed will cost you your job.''

With a flurry of silk the older woman turned and stalked away, unaware of the rude gesture that followed her.

''Excuse me,'' Amanda said tentatively.

The plump young woman glanced at Amanda, then back to her clipboard as though she would find a clue to Amanda's appearance listed there.

''Okay, I've got it,'' the woman said after a moment. ''You're Amanda Timbers. Steve called to say you were on your way up.'' Shoving the clipboard under her arm, she extended her hand. ''I'm Ginny Denver. Oates has the day off and I've been delegated to get you settled in—along with everything else,'' she added under her breath.

Glancing around, she called out. ''Ralph, will you get Amanda's bags?'' She turned back to Amanda and extended her hand. ''He'll need your keys.'' After handing the keys to a tall, slouching man, she said, ''Take them to four West.''

Ginny shoved a hand through her flyaway hair. ''What first? Your room,'' she said answering her own question as she walked away. ''The west wing is through this hall. It'll probably be a little confusing for you at first, but you'll get used to it.'' She moved quickly, barely allowing Amanda to keep up. ''There are four wings of bedrooms. East, West, A-North and B-North. But we don't usually call them that. You'll learn the nicknames soon enough.''

When Amanda laughed aloud, Ginny slowed down and glanced at her quizzically, a reluctant smile curving her full lips. "What did I say that's funny?"

"Don't you ever slow down?"

"Not very often," she said wryly as she reached a staircase and took the first step. "Especially when Oates is away. I have seniority, God help me."

Now that she had the opportunity, Amanda took it. "Who is Oates? And are you the social director and who is Steve and what does Ralph do other than carry luggage?"

Ginny laughed. "Oates is Mrs. Beryl Oates, officially the housekeeper, unofficially the warden. I'm a nurse, but we all have to dress like this. Oates tries to convince us we're all one big happy family. And more important, she feels the guests will feel more at ease if we dress casually." She pinched up her mouth. "'We want to convey the feeling that we are all guests of a wealthy gentleman.'" She rolled her eyes. "If I ever visit a wealthy gentleman, I'll lie in bed the whole time. Steve is the guard at the gate, and Ralph is general handyman. Anything else?"

Amanda felt as though she should be taking notes. "What about Dr. Sutherland?" she asked tentatively. "Does he live here?"

"He has a private apartment here—you should see his dining room. Looks like something out of the White House," Ginny said in a wry aside. "But he's only here off and on. He has a house in Beverly Hills and an apartment in New York."

They were now in a wide carpeted hall with doors on each side like an apartment building. "And this one big happy family bit?'' Amanda asked. ''Just exactly what does that mean?''

Ginny gave her a shrewd look. ''You're a book-keeper, right?''

Amanda nodded.

''Wrong, O Innocent One. Here you are whatever is needed. We never stick to our job description. Although we have regular shifts, we're on call twenty-four hours a day and everyone pitches in during a crisis.''

Amanda glanced at her warily. ''Are there very many crises?''

Ginny shrugged. ''About the same as you would find in any family of forty overgrown children.''

''There are forty...guests?''

She nodded. ''About twenty-five residents and fifteen transients, as we call them. They just pass through.''

Stopping in front of a door, Ginny opened it and preceded Amanda inside. The room was bright and airy and big enough to hold a small sitting area. Although the furniture was not of the same quality that had been in the lounge, it wasn't bad; it was the type one would find in a mid-price hotel. Amanda had expected something along the lines of ''early motel''—lots of plastic and garish prints.

Glancing around approvingly she said, ''Not exactly your average employee's bedroom.''

''This is not exactly your average health farm.''

''Yes, I can see that.'' Moving to the window, she stared out, trying to get her bearings. She had somehow thought the window would look out on the front lawns. But the landscape she saw was completely different.

"You can see the small swimming pool from here," Ginny said as she leaned against a dark, highly polished bureau. She raised one foot to flex it, then the other. "The big one—Olympic-size—is on the other side of B-North. Employees share the small pool with the loonies, and the transients share with the old-timers. Each wing except ours has a private garden surrounded by a nine-foot hedge. To your right are the tennis courts and beyond that the stables. Greenleigh has one hundred and twenty acres in all, some beautiful bridle and footpaths, duck ponds and semi-natural streams."

"Hold it," Amanda said, trying to catch her breath. "You're going too fast again. You sound like a freaked-out travelogue."

"Sorry," Ginny said, grimacing. "They've been coming at me all day. I think there's some rule that says if you're rich you have to have the personality of a gorilla in rut. If you don't, they come and take your money away."

"You said loonies," Amanda said, staring at her in confusion. "Does that mean you have mental patients here? I thought this was some kind of hot-stuff spa for the very wealthy."

"It is, but the rich have their nuts, too. Haven't you ever wondered where they put them?"

"I can't say that I have."

"The loonies—which is cruel but typical of the mentality around here—are the ones who really need psychiatric care. They're in B-North, right there." She moved to stand beside Amanda and gestured to a wing that angled away from them. "A-North is the old-timers' wing. They're permanent residents; for them this is a fancy old-folks' home. My parents should have it so good."

Glancing at her watch, Ginny moved away from the window. "Now that you've seen your room, we'd better look at the rest of it—at least the important parts. I hate to rush you, but lunch is coming up, and there are always squabbles over who gets which table."

Several minutes later, they were back in the lounge. Amanda hadn't noticed before how many doors opened off of it. Would she ever learn her way around?

They paused before one of the open doors, and Ginny nodded toward the interior. "The dining room."

Amanda stepped past her to look inside. Deep-red carpet covered the floors giving contrast to the massive chandeliers that hung magestically from the ceiling. There were numerous small tables draped with startlingly white linen cloths. Crystal and silver were already in place, and floral centerpieces decorated each table.

"The guests can eat here if they feel sociable or they can eat in their rooms. We have a Belgian chef who is very temperamental about being asked for a soufflé at three in the morning, but Dr. Sutherland pays him well so he keeps his grousing to himself," Ginny said dryly. "He also caters the doctor's dinner parties. The doctor's private dining room seats twenty, and it's by invitation only. Sometimes he gets up a party but only for very special guests.''

When Ginny spoke of Dr. Sutherland her voice softened and her brown eyes sparkled. Amanda couldn't blame the nurse; the one time she had met the doctor, her own pulse had picked up a bit. Even if Amanda had been able to overlook his stunning appearance, she had almost overdosed on the charm that positively oozed from him.

Before Dr. Anderson had told her about the job at Greenleigh Acres, Amanda had heard of Ted Sutherland. Anyone who watched television at all had heard of him. Talk-show hosts loved him. Although his reputation as a doctor hadn't hurt, Amanda suspected it had been his charm and playboy reputation that had prompted a recent Barbara Walters special on him.

Leaving the dining room, they passed several other open doors. Amanda got tantalizing glimpses of grand pianos in one and walls of plants and glass in another. She hoped she could find them again when she had time to explore.

They entered another hall. "The old-timers' rooms are above the offices," Ginny said, stopping in front of a door. "This is your office. Oates is next door and Cherry—Dr. Sutherland's secretary—has one just down the hall."

It didn't look like any office Amanda had ever worked in. With its dark paneled walls and leather furniture and small fireplace, it looked like a wealthy man's study—maybe one of his lesser studies, the place where he received menials or mistresses rather than heads of state.

Walking across the room, Ginny slid open a wooden panel to reveal built-in filing cabinets. "Here are all the files—at least the financial ones, insurance and that kind of thing. The medical files are kept in Dr. Sutherland's secretary's office or in the basement where he does his research."

"He has a research lab here?"

"Are you kidding? Some hospitals don't have such sophisticated labs. I'll show it to you sometime," Ginny said over her shoulder as she pulled back burgundy-colored drapes to let in the sunlight.

Amanda walked to the window and looked out, then shook her head, trying to take everything in. Her head was whirling with all the visual and verbal information.

"Think you'll like it?" Ginny asked from behind her. "You look a little stunned, as though it's not quite what you expected. Didn't you check it out before you applied for the job?"

"Actually I didn't apply for it," Amanda said ruefully. "Dr. Anderson—I worked for him for the past six years at a small clinic in Los Angeles—decided to retire, but being the man he is, he wanted to make sure I had somewhere to go. He talked to Dr. Sutherland, which led to an interview, which led me here." She shrugged. "It's all a little confusing. I thought this was a fancy kind of dude ranch. I had no idea it was an institution."

"Greenleigh Acres is unique," Ginny said, and not without a hint of pride in her voice. "It's not a hospital or a funny farm. Mostly it's a resting place for the rich and famous. We get actors and actresses who want to lose weight or dry out or who are simply between pictures and need pampering. In fact Delores Carey is here right now.''

Amanda swung around. ''Really?'' she asked, impressed against her will as she thought of the auburn-haired actress who had been the top box-office draw of the sixties. ''She's one of my favorite actresses. I must have seen *The Dark Backward* a dozen times.''

Ginny grimaced. ''Don't worry. You'll meet her. No one escapes Miss Carey unnoticed. We also get actresses who are on their way to being somebody. Protégées of directors or other rich men. They come here to recuperate from nose jobs or breast augmentation or tummy tucks or having the fat sucked out of them.'' Ginny leaned against the desk. ''And sometimes Greenleigh is simply a place for the pillars of society to send their embarrassments.''

''Embarrassments?''

''We get a lot of those—I won't call them loonies because I can tell it upsets you; you'll toughen up in time. Right now we've got a twenty-year-old man who enjoys dressing in women's clothes. The catch is his father is a famous senator. And we have Mrs. Osgood. Her nephew is big in computers. That's not exactly a sensitive occupation, but he's trying to get the government to institute reforms in public education. Her 'eccentricities' would set him back a century. And then there's Virgie.''

''Virgie?''

''DeVries. You've heard the name, of course.''

"Not as in William DeVries?" Amanda said, picturing the strong, down-to-earth face of the world-famous evangelist.

"The same," Ginny said. "Virgie, his daughter, likes men...too much. She's a nympho like you've never seen before. She's caused us no end of problems. She's hit on every man on staff and not a few of the guests."

Amanda swallowed heavily. What in hell had Dr. Anderson gotten her into? "Tell me about the rest of the staff," she said, trying to get the conversation back to territory familiar to her.

"Let's see," Ginny said, flopping down on the couch. "We have a total of ten nurses—you'll meet them all later—at least three on duty at all times. Dr. Greg Nabors is the internist who takes care of things when Dr. Sutherland is away. Resident psychiatrist, Paul Choate. A full staff in the kitchen. Maids, gardeners, lifeguards, stable personnel and guards." She ticked them off on her fingers.

"Guards?"

"That's mostly to keep reporters and nosy people out," Ginny said. "We rarely have any trouble inside, but sometimes one of the loonies will get testy. That's when the guards come in handy."

The door opened and a tall, harassed-looking redhead stuck her head in. "Ginny, I've been looking everywhere for you. Mrs. Baxter is doing it again," she said, her voice breathless. "In the lounge."

"Oh, hell," Ginny said, pulling herself to her feet. "Come on, Amanda. Time for your baptism by fire."

She moved quickly toward the door with Amanda two paces behind her. "Who is Mrs. Baxter, and what is she doing in the lounge?" Amanda asked, trying to keep up with the rapidly moving nurse.

"Evelyn Baxter, and if she's holding true to form, she's putting on a show for the guests," Ginny said over her shoulder, her voice husky with exertion. "She used to be one of the most famous socialites in Palm Beach. Her husband, with his brothers, owns Baxter's Department Stores. Evelyn's husband didn't like the way she was treating his mistress, so he had her shipped here."

"Can he do that legally?"

Ginny shrugged. "Since Evelyn tried to drown said mistress by pushing her face into a bowl of champagne punch, he was probably being kind."

They ran the rest of the way. When they reached the lounge, they heard laughter and saw a crowd of people gathered to one side of the room. Suddenly a purple silk blouse came flying over the top of the crowd. It landed gently on the head of a portly bald man, the color clashing violently with his orange plaid Bermuda shorts.

When Ginny began pushing her way through the onlookers, Amanda followed because it seemed to be expected of her. At the center, a thin, middle-aged woman that Amanda presumed was Mrs. Baxter stood with her hands on her hips, still wearing a lavender satin slip. Her platinum hair hung in a smooth pageboy the way it must have done for years. Outsize, tinted, rimless glasses covered the upper part of her face. She had a look Amanda had seen before, but only in Beverly Hills and on Rodeo Drive.

The older woman laughed throatily and continued to back away from the people cautiously approaching her. Suddenly, she turned and ran. She was surprisingly agile for her age. Like Hamlin's helpless children, everyone followed her across the lounge, then down a hall, watching helplessly as she ducked through swinging doors.

"The kitchen," Ginny said over her shoulders to Amanda as she, too, pushed open the doors.

The kitchen gleamed with stainless steel and white porcelain. The white-uniformed staff was gathered together in a corner, talking casually to each other, waiting for the disruption to be taken care of as though it were an entirely normal, and even expected, event.

"Evelyn," Ginny called coaxingly. "Come on now, put that down."

In one hand, Evelyn Baxter held a massive strawberry shortcake, a creation that should have been in a gallery above a plaque stating "Sculpture in Red and White." The older woman lowered her gaze to the confection, then raised it slowly to the people just inside the door, her eyes sparkling. Before anyone had time to prepare for her next move, the beautiful dessert came sailing through the air.

And the battle was on. Amanda caught her breath and ducked behind a table, noticing that others were also taking cover. *I've stepped through the looking glass,* she thought, feeling a giggle rise to the surface as chiffon pies and cream puffs landed with soft splats around her.

Gathering her courage, she peeked over the table just as a napoleon hit a tall man in the stomach. Mrs. Baxter shrieked and jumped in the air victoriously, for all the world like a cheerleader at a football game.

Amanda laughed. She couldn't help it. Everyone was taking it so seriously while Mrs. Baxter was so obviously enjoying herself. If Evelyn Baxter was an example of the mental patients at Greenleigh Acres, Amanda knew she had nothing to worry about. The older woman was simply a mischievous elf.

To one side of the door, Ginny whispered to Ralph, obviously planning their battle strategy. Amanda glanced back at Mrs. Baxter and caught her breath.

"Oh, no," she whispered, then she shouted. "Ginny, watch out! For heaven's sake...duck."

The last word came out sheepishly as a lemon chiffon pie glanced off the side of Ginny's face. The pale-yellow mass slid slowly downward, catching in the brown hair, dripping to the tennis dress.

Amanda sank back to her hiding place behind the table, hoping Ginny wasn't looking in her direction to see her shaking with laughter.

Then suddenly Amanda's laughter died as she met gray eyes across the room. Laughing gray eyes. Now there were three of them in the room enjoying the scene, Amanda thought with pleasure. There was an immediate sense of recognition, of déjà vu. It was wonderful, like climbing an icy mountain and suddenly coming across edelweiss.

In those few seconds it was as though she and the man with the gray eyes had spoken aloud, their conversation leaving her strangely exhilarated. She knew this was a man she would like. This was a man she wanted to know better.

Maybe he was the psychiatrist, Choate, she thought. He was well over six feet tall, large-framed, looking more like a boxer than a doctor, and was casually dressed, but so was everyone else.

As Amanda watched, another man approached the one with the laughing eyes. The gray-eyed man's smile faded and the two men walked away together. As the door closed behind them, she decided that maybe her old boss, Dr. Anderson, had known what he was doing after all when he retired.

Smiling, her attention returned to the kitchen carnage. Two guards were braving the sticky missiles and approaching Mrs. Baxter. Amanda had the feeling that the older woman had decided on her own that the game was over or they wouldn't have taken her so easily. As they walked away, the men slipped and slid on the glutinous mess, trying to look dignified and failing.

As the door swung shut, Mrs. Baxter's voice drifted back like lingering smoke on an empty battlefield. "Oh, my, that was fun," she said. "Let's do it again tomorrow."

When Amanda moved to stand beside Ginny, the nurse glanced up, her eyes daring Amanda to comment. "I'm sorry," Amanda said, laughter bubbling up again. "I know it's awful, but Ginny, you look so funny. There's a little blob of whipped cream just above your ear."

Ginny stared at her for a moment, eyes narrow, then slowly she began to chuckle. "Okay, it's funny...from the outside. You ought to try it from this side."

On their way back to the office, Amanda said, "Ginny, who was the tall man by the door?"

"Who?"

"The one with the unusual gray eyes," Amanda said. "I thought maybe it was the psychiatrist."

"Paul has brown eyes." Ginny touched up her hair gingerly and grimaced. "I've got to go clean up. This is definitely not in my contract. If you'll stay here, I'll take you to lunch when I get back."

When the door closed behind the nurse, Amanda moved to sit behind the wooden desk. Her first day on the job, she thought, giving her head a wry shake. Then she laughed softly. If this was any indication of what was to come, at least she wouldn't be bored.

Looking through the desk drawer, she began to decide where she would put her things. Pictures, pen-and-ink set, all the things that would truly make this her office.

Her office, she thought with a grin as she leaned back in the leather chair to prop her feet on the desk. Her last office had been a beige cubbyhole. Beige furniture, beige carpet and beige work. The work here would be positively psychedelic in comparison.

She almost fell over backward when the door opened and Dr. Sutherland walked in. Jumping up, she nervously smoothed her linen skirt. "Dr. Sutherland," she said, her voice husky with surprise.

He smiled. "Sit down. You look good there."

The owner of Greenleigh was tanned and slender, looking more like an artist than a doctor. His features were breathtakingly perfect. But it was the soft charismatic smile that captured attention.

"I'm sorry I wasn't here to welcome you, Amanda," he said, his accent leaning toward Boston. "I hear Mrs. Baxter has created a stir. Not a very good introduction to Greenleigh Acres, I'm afraid," he added with what sounded like genuine regret.

Her blue eyes sparkled with laughter. "I didn't mind. It made me feel like one of the family. I'm glad to see the guests enjoy themselves."

There was no answering smile in his eyes as he leaned one hip against her desk. "Mrs. Baxter is something of a problem," he said, his voice serious. "But after all, that's what Greenleigh is here for. I'm just sorry it happened on your first day. I should have been here to introduce you to the facilities."

"Please, don't apologize, Dr. Sutherland," she said, feeling vaguely uncomfortable. He obviously took his work seriously. "I know you're a busy man. I honestly didn't expect you to take care of me."

"You're a member of the family now," he said, flashing the charming smile at her again. "Call me Ted." When he reached out and took her hand, she blushed in her confusion. "I hope you haven't gained a bad opinion of us. It's usually peaceful here."

She murmured a denial, wondering what on earth was wrong with her. She was definitely flattered by his attention. After all, he had the most beautiful women on two coasts drooling over him. But this was not the kind of employer-employee relationship she was used to. While she had no objection to seeing him after working hours, she preferred an uncomplicated atmosphere in the office.

As though sensing her hesitancy, he rose and walked toward the door. "I'll leave you to get settled in now. But if there are any problems, just come to me."

"Dr. Sutherland?" He lifted a brow. "Ted," she amended, laughing hesitantly. "There was a man in the kitchen." She smiled apologetically. "I'm trying to get the staff straight in my mind," she explained. "He was tall, muscular. Dark hair. Dimple in his chin. Scar on his forehead."

He thought for a moment. "I don't really...wait, you must have seen Daniel Phillips."

Daniel Phillips, she thought. A nice name. "What's his position here?"

"He doesn't work here," he said, grasping for the doorknob. "He's a guest at Greenleigh Acres."

Amanda held her breath. As her pulse picked up, she almost knew what was coming.

"Until recently he was a leader in world industry, but unfortunately he is a victim of Sutherland's Complex." He said the words matter-of-factly, his voice clinical and detached. "It's left him hopelessly brain-damaged."

Chapter Two

As though hypnotized, Amanda watched the door close behind him, then sat down slowly. Glancing down at her hands, she was surprised to find them shaking. She was shocked, more shocked than seemed reasonable.

Daniel Phillips's face rose up before her. His laughing eyes, his strong stubborn jaw. This and what she'd just learned were certainly incongruous, but she had never met the man. Why was she so distressed to find that he was brain-damaged?

Biting her lip, she tried to shake the feeling. Maybe it was the job itself rather than Daniel Phillips that was worrying her. In her old job, Amanda had been separate from individuals. They had merely been statistics, facts and figures in a paper file. When she had closed out a file, logically she had known that someone had died, but she had not known him or her personally. She had never once encountered the hopelessness of disease or disability.

Not only had she never encountered it in her job, Amanda thought suddenly; she had never encountered it in her personal life. It was something of a shock to realize that she had never known any physically or mentally handicapped people. That seemed wrong somehow. Were they so segregated that she had never come across any? Or, more disturbing still, had she unconsciously avoided them?

Amanda cut her thoughts off sharply when the door opened and Ginny walked in. The nurse had changed into a bright orange sundress that no more suited her coloring than had the tennis dress.

"Lunchtime," Ginny said cheerfully, evidently having disposed of the Baxter incident along with the lemon pie. "I'll introduce you to more of the staff now."

In the dining room, they took a table overlooking a small garden. The white-jacketed waiter took their order just as though they were patrons of an exclusive restaurant. After all that had happened, it felt a little like sitting down at the Mad Hatter's table for tea.

Amanda played with the silver knife for a while, her mind strangely sluggish as she thought back over everything that had happened since her arrival. Inhaling slowly, she glanced up. "Ginny, who is Daniel Phillips?"

"Danny?" Ginny asked. "Did you meet him? He's a love, isn't he?"

"I didn't actually meet him. I'm just interested. Tell me about him. He looks so... so normal."

"He looks like a hunk," Ginny said. "He's been here about six months. And he's one of the most gentle people I've ever known...as long as he gets his medication."

Amanda frowned. "What happens if he doesn't get his medication?"

"It's only happened once," she said. "It was a new nurse—I don't even remember her name. She didn't stay long enough to become an old nurse. Danny has to receive his medication every twelve hours. The nurse was busy, and by the time she got around to him, the effects of his last dose was wearing off. It took four guards and two nurses to hold him down. A lot of people had bruises the next day."

"You mean he becomes violent," Amanda asked, trying to relate these facts to the man she had seen in the kitchen.

"Violent is too mild a word," Ginny said, giving her a wry look. "He was out to do murder. But don't let it worry you. I'm in charge of his medication now, so there will be no more mistakes."

Amanda shrugged helplessly, wondering again why it mattered so much. "You would never guess to look at him that he was... that there was anything wrong with him."

Ginny raised one slender eyebrow. "Did you expect him to drool or something?" she asked, her tone causing Amanda to shift uncomfortably. "You'll get used to it. You treat the transients like the Queen Mother; you treat the Special Ones and the old-timers like children. After a couple of weeks, all this will seem normal to you."

Amanda laughed. "When this seems normal, I'll be ready for a room in B-North myself." She shook her head. "But since I want to keep this job, I'll pretend to accept everything. Even the fact that the man with the laughing gray eyes is really a patient. That one may be a little tough."

"Wait until you get to know him. After a while, you won't remember your first reaction to him. He's thirty-nine, tests out at about a six-year-old level. And, like a six-year-old, he can ask some of the most damnable questions. They have no diplomacy at that age."

This is weird, Amanda thought, her confusion reflected in her eyes. The whole setup was weird. "Why do you call him one of the Special Ones? Who are the Special Ones?"

"The ones with Sutherland's Complex," Ginny said, picking up a fork as the waiter set their salads before them. "We only have two right now—um, this is good—Danny, and Maribel Fortnoy. Haven't you heard of the complex? It's been written up in all the medical journals and even some of the popular science magazines."

Amanda shook her head. "I suppose it has something to do with Ted . . . Dr. Sutherland."

Ginny nodded. "It's his life's work. His wife died ten years ago of a degenerative brain disorder, not Sutherland's Complex, but in his research to find out more about her disease he discovered the complex.

That's the reason for the lab in the basement. He drives himself too hard."

So Ginny had a crush on Ted, Amanda thought, watching the nurse's face as she spoke. Amanda couldn't really blame her. He was definitely out of the ordinary.

"Hello."

Amanda turned to see a man of slight build standing beside the table. His red hair curled attractively, framing his lean, intelligent face. Amanda smiled up at him, then glanced at the woman across the table.

"Amanda, this is Paul Choate, our resident psychiatrist." Ginny's voice was stiff, her expression aloof. "Amanda is our new bookkeeper."

Reaching out to clasp the extended hand, Amanda said, "It's nice to meet you, Paul." He had a strong handshake. She liked that.

"Same here," he said, smiling shyly. "You're very welcome at Greenleigh. The last bookkeeper was chunky and male and bit his nails."

She laughed, glancing at her hands. "I don't bite my nails, but I'm sure I have habits that are just as annoying." She looked at him warily. "I hope you don't secretly analyze the people you work with."

He grinned. "Occupational hazard, I'm afraid," he said, ruefully. He fell silent, staring at Ginny expectantly as though waiting for an invitation to join them. As the nurse stared determinedly at her water glass, the tension built. Then Paul smiled sadly and walked away with a murmured goodbye.

Amanda stared at Ginny. "He seems nice," she said tentatively. "And very attractive."

"Forget it," Ginny said brusquely. "He prefers blondes."

Suddenly she stiffened and Amanda followed her gaze to the doorway of the dining room. A very blond, very sexy woman had just entered the room. Her very-wealthy-woman-lounging-around-the-house outfit was blue, complementing her tanned limbs. She was gorgeous, but she was also very self-conscious in the way Charlotte Brontë meant the word, conscious of the way her body moved, the way her blond hair made the perfect frame for her face.

"Who's that?" Amanda whispered, leaning forward. "She looks like a movie star."

"Leah Houseman." Ginny's lips were tight with disapproval. "She's supposed to be our physical therapist."

The blonde moved across the room, attracting not a little attention, and sat at a table with a man who looked like a male model. There was a flash of white, even teeth in an evenly tanned male face.

"And that's Greg Nabors, our internist."

"They make quite a couple," Amanda murmured.

"She and every man within reach make quite a couple," Ginny said. "She knows them all ... and I mean in the biblical sense. Right now she's having a supposedly secret affair with Tom Dicks. Secret only because she considers him beneath her socially. Of course, it's the physical that she's after. She's been through everyone else. She has her sights set on Dr. Sutherland, but he's too discriminating to sleep with her. It makes me sick to my stomach that Virgie is in here as a patient when Leah, who is no better, is staff."

Amanda bit her lip. She could hear the hatred in Ginny's voice and it made her uncomfortable. "Who is Tom Dicks?" she asked in an effort to turn the conversation away from Leah Houseman.

"Hmm? Oh, he's the man who takes care of Danny," Ginny said, her voice distracted as she stared at her salad. "You'll probably meet him later."

As they fell into an uneasy silence, Amanda gazed around the room. Very soon she was almost sure she could spot which of the diners were employees. Turning to Ginny, she said, "This may sound vain, but is it a prerequisite for employees to be attractive?"

Ginny glanced up. "I'd never thought of it before, but I guess it is. That's probably why the old bookkeeper didn't last. The people who come here are rich enough to buy beauty. Heaven forbid that they should see a plain face taking their temperatures or cleaning up their messes."

They ate in silence for a while. Suddenly, Ginny laid down her fork noisily. "I'm not really hungry," she said, her voice gruff as she avoided Amanda's eyes. "And I'll bet you're exhausted. Why don't you go take a nap? You don't start work until tomorrow. You might as well take advantage of the free time."

It didn't take a genius to know Ginny wanted to be alone. Amanda left her outside the dining room and made her way back to her room. But she didn't want to rest. She was too keyed up. Too much was happening too soon.

Moving to the window, she looked over the grounds. The pool's blue water sparkled in the sunlight. Short palms lined the edges, giving it a touch of

Hollywood that seemed redundant given the beautiful people seated under umbrellas and reclining in loungers.

It looked inviting. Making up her mind quickly, she changed into a white, one-piece suit and grabbed a towel. A few minutes later, she stood on the edge of the pool. Inhaling, she dived in and swam the length several times, then held on to the side to catch her breath.

Boy, are you out of shape, she told herself. Not so long ago she could have swum the length ten times and not even felt the strain.

"The white suit looks nice, dear, but with that hair, a teal-blue bikini would be outstanding."

Amanda jerked her head up and saw the face she had seen so often on the screen of a darkened theater gazing at her with those famous drooping, sexy eyes.

Delores Carey was still beautiful. The fact that she had gone slightly zaftig didn't affect her famous sensuality one whit. Her red hair was hidden by an outrageous flowered bathing cap that matched the sarong-type swimsuit molding her ample curves.

"Miss Carey," Amanda said, smiling in pleasure. "It doesn't really matter, does it? With you here, no one would notice if I were wearing fig leaves."

The older woman laughed. "I like you. Come out and talk to me."

Pulling herself up to sit on the side of the pool, Amanda grabbed the towel she had brought from her room and blotted her long hair. Then she moved to sit on the adjacent lounger.

"Would it be gauche to say I've seen every movie you've ever done and loved them all?"

"Only if you add that you saw them all on the late, late show."

"I don't suppose a Delores Carey revival would be less offensive?" Amanda asked, laughing.

"Only slightly." She sighed. "Don't ever get old—what's your name?"

"Amanda...Amanda Timbers. I'm the new bookkeeper."

"What an amazingly dull occupation for someone with your looks," she said dryly. "Well, Amanda, as I was saying, never get old. Do yourself in at the age of twenty-nine. Old age is a self-inflicted wound."

"You don't look over twenty-nine, but if the daily tabloids are right, you are. But that didn't keep you from getting the Oscar for *The Dark Backward*, which happens to be my favorite movie of all time."

"I played an aging hooker," Delores said. "What kind of role was that? If they hadn't had to apply makeup to make me look older, more dissipated, I'd never have taken it."

"You loved it," Amanda said accusingly. "I can tell by your voice."

Delores laughed. "You're right. I loved it. I think I was finally playing myself."

"I don't believe that, but you were wonderful anyway. Are you between pictures? Is that why you're here?"

"How kind of you. I am probably permanently between pictures. The only ones offered now are the kind that have me playing some sweet old lady who buries people in her petunia bed or hangs them neatly in the cellar. No, I'm here because of a chronic condition. You laymen call it loneliness. I just got rid of gorgeous young stud number nine hundred and seventy-eight. Actually he got rid of me, but I don't pine for him."

"I'm sorry."

"Don't be. All men are snots, but I'm sure you know that. And age has nothing to do with it. There are simply young snots and old snots. This one I don't miss at all. No foreplay, absolutely none," she said, leaning toward Amanda. "The only thing he had going for him was enthusiasm—youth is so vigorous—and the size of his—"

Amanda gave a choking cough. "I think we can leave the rest to my imagination," she said, laughing. "What are you doing at this pool? I thought there was one on the other side that the guests use."

"There is, complete with manufactured waterfall. But they're all so boring over there. The most interesting conversation I would get there is what type of spoon to use with caviar," she said, her voice malicious. "Silver gives the caviar a metallic taste, you understand. It must be mother-of-pearl or nothing."

"I don't think I've ever seen a mother-of-pearl spoon," Amanda said, enjoying the conversation. "Why couldn't you use stainless steel?"

"It wouldn't leave a metallic taste, of course. But, my dear Amanda, consider the aesthetics," she said, raising her perfect nose. When Amanda laughed, Delores said, "No, I much prefer the employees and the loonies." She waved to a man walking toward them.

"And so does John. Don't you, darling?" she said as he joined them.

"Don't I what?"

At first glance, the man lowering himself to a chair on the other side of Delores looked to be in his mid-fifties, but on closer observation Amanda saw the fragility of age beneath the surface. He was probably in his seventies but still very attractive. With his iron-gray hair and hawklike nose, he would stand out in any crowd.

"Don't you prefer to be with the employees and the loonies rather than the obnoxious bunch of people staff calls the guests?" Delores asked.

Amanda thought she saw him wince at Delores's phrasing, but then he said, "I prefer to be anyplace where there are beautiful women." He eyed the actress lasciviously. "Now introduce me to the lovely mermaid."

"This is Amanda Timbers. She's the new book-keeper, but right now she's entertaining me. Amanda, this is Mr. John J. Pike. Tycoon *extraordinaire*. Watch out for him, dear, he pinches."

"Lies. Vicious lies. I do much more patting than I do pinching."

Delores rose. "Time for me to take a swim."

"You only do it because you know we all enjoy watching you," John accused.

"That's true," she said before stepping gingerly into the water.

"You look slightly star struck," John said, smiling at Amanda.

She turned to him. "That's the way I feel. She's wonderful."

"You'll get no argument from me." He leaned back in the padded chair. "And how do you like Greenleigh so far?"

"I haven't been here long enough to get my bearings. So far it's been very exciting. Ginny said I'll come to think of it all as normal." She laughed. "Even if there were no people, the sheer luxury of the place would be overwhelming."

"It's fancy all right," he said, his voice dry.

"John J. Pike!"

They both turned. Amanda sucked in her breath as she watched Danny walk toward them. The black bathing suit he wore exposed the hard strength she had only suspected in the kitchen. He looked tough, but symmetrical, a streetwise Hercules.

As he drew nearer Amanda studied his face, searching for a key that would pull everything together. She needed some point of reference. But there was nothing, nothing that told her he was incomplete.

When he reached them, he sat cross-legged on the tile beside the lounge chairs. "John J. Pike, you promised—"

"Manners, Danny," John said. "I want to introduce you to Amanda Timbers. She'll be living here. Amanda, this is Daniel Phillips."

His face was solemn as he extended his hand. His grip was strong. "Hello," he said quietly.

"Hello, Danny."

He kept her hand in his, his gaze traveling slowly over her body then back to her face. She could feel his gaze on each feature, taking in the slim, straight nose, the dark, wide-set eyes, lingering on the fullness of her lower lip.

She was relieved when he released her hand at last and turned back to John. "She's very pretty," he said.

John laughed. "That she is, Danny. That she is," he agreed. "I take it you're ready for that swimming match?"

Danny nodded, his gray eyes steady.

Amanda stared after them as they walked away. Sooner or later she would accept his disability, she assured herself. She had to. She didn't know why it was so important; she only knew that it was.

"God, that Danny is gorgeous."

Amanda glanced up to see Delores drying off with an enormous pink towel as she watched Danny execute a perfect dive into the pool.

"Sometimes I find myself flirting with him before I remember," she said, lighting a long, brown cigarette. "Then he'll say something totally young and disarming and I feel like a dirty old woman."

"I'm sure he enjoys talking to you," Amanda said, staring at her hands. She didn't want to talk about Danny; she didn't even want to think of him. "Have you been at Greenleigh long?"

"Only about two weeks. There's a whole new batch of people here. John is an old friend and most of the staff is the same, but Danny is new and so are several others in B-North. You see that young man in the green bathing suit?" Amanda glanced at the other side of the pool, then nodded. "I think he became too fond of his English sheepdog."

"Delores!" Amanda gasped. "How do you know that?"

"I don't," she said as though that didn't matter. "I made it up, but look at him. Doesn't he look a prime candidate for bestiality? I had a butler once—"

"Please," Amanda said, laughing weakly. "Don't tell me about your butler. Aren't there any people here who don't have deviant vices?"

Delores looked down her nose as only Delores could do. "Why on earth do you think I come here? The most interesting people in the country are here."

"Since you're here, I'll accept that."

"Me? No, I'm afraid not. Haven't you noticed that all the really insightful, really profound women of the past century have been gay?" She shook her head in regret. "And I am so determinedly heterosexual, I despair of ever being truly interesting."

Amanda laughed. She had never heard anything so outrageous said so beautifully. "You're wrong. You're totally interesting, deviant or not."

"Deviant is in the eye of the beholder," Delores said, stretching luxuriously, "just as normal is. Oh, God, Virgie and Peter are fighting again."

The two people who had captured Delores's attention were standing at the end of the pool, both young and attractive, both shouting violently. The girl, her black hair pulled up in a knot on top of her head, was small but curvaceous, the pink bikini she wore leaving almost nothing to the imagination. The young man with her was only a few inches taller and looked slightly emaciated.

"They just naturally rub each other the wrong way," Delores said. "You would think their problems would cause a bond—given the similarity."

Amanda was not a natural gossip; it made her uncomfortable. But she had the distinct feeling that she was about to gossip whether she liked it or not. She was right.

"Virgie is a nympho," Delores said casually, lying back on the lounge chair. "And Peter is a drug addict. They kicked him out of medical school because of it.

"Virgie! Peter!" she called, waving to get their attention. Virgie responded with a digital gesture that made Delores laugh. Peter turned away from the girl and walked toward them. He looked extremely young and vulnerable, but as he drew closer, Amanda saw that his eyes were old. Old and sad and cynical.

"Hello, Has-Been," he said as he reached them.

"Hello, Junkie," Delores responded, laughing throatily.

Staring down at Delores, he studied her famous features. "I don't suppose you've read the Robert Frost poem about aged actresses, have you? His advice was to buy a few friends to keep you company in your later years." He raised a brow in inquiry. "I haven't seen a penny."

"And you won't," she said firmly. "Now stop being a show-off and meet Amanda, new member of the family. She's into books."

"So you're a literary person," Peter said as he sat down. "A lot of you seem to go around the bend."

"Not that kind of book, I'm afraid," Amanda said. "I'm a bookkeeper, and I think it's too dull a profession to cause many breakdowns."

"No, you're right. Bookkeepers always skip to South America with the money."

As he spoke, Peter watched Virgie from the corner of his eyes. His face grew stormy as she pulled off the top of her bikini and threw it to a group of cheering young men. "Everyone has problems," he said, his voice moody. "I think the world would be a lot better off if we were all insensitive, unintelligent boobs. It's the sensitive ones who always pay."

Amanda shivered. She was almost glad when John and Danny returned.

"I'll have to leave you all now," John said. "Nabors finds me so interesting, he insists on checking me every day. It was nice meeting you, Amanda. I hope you enjoy working here."

"We were supposed to go horseback riding," Danny said when John had gone. "Do you think John J. Pike is getting old?"

"We all get old, Danny," Peter said. "But don't worry about John. He'll probably outlast all of us. I'd offer to go riding with you, but I have an appointment with the shrink. When I'm late he makes me talk about my pubescent years to punish me."

Amanda watched Peter stand, then caught the look in Danny's eyes. It was not disappointment; it was emptiness.

"I could go riding with you." The words were out of her mouth before she realized what was happening. She immediately bit her lip.

Danny turned to her. "Do you ride?" he said, his voice soft and slow and slightly hesitant. "Really ride? Miss Carey says she rides, but she doesn't. She won't even let her horse trot."

"You ungrateful wretch," Delores said. "I spent an hour on that stupid animal last week."

Danny gazed at her earnestly. "You looked awfully... awfully pretty in your riding clothes."

Delores leaned down and kissed him on the cheek, then glanced at Amanda. "They're born knowing how to handle women. Watch out for him. He'll have you cleaning the stables or something equally revolting if you're not careful."

"Can you really ride?" Danny asked again, turning back to Amanda.

"Yes, I really can," she said in resignation. "Give me thirty minutes to get dressed and I'll show you. Where should we meet?"

"At the stables," he said, standing, his eyes warm with pleasure.

She inhaled slowly and forced a smile. "Okay, it's a date."

Chapter Three

Why in hell had she offered to go with him? Amanda's movements were stiff and awkward as she made her way to the stables. This was all she needed, she thought, to be babysitter for a—a...oh hell, she didn't even know how to describe him in her thoughts. She swung her dark hair around impatiently. She had pulled it up in a ponytail and was dressed in jeans, T-shirt and riding boots.

As she neared the stable, she saw Danny waiting beside two horses. He, too, had changed into riding clothes, only his looked like something Prince Charles would wear to play polo. She glanced away quickly from the hard, attractive body.

"I told Max to give you Ariadne," he said, his voice soft and husky. As he spoke, he didn't take his eyes from her and the intensity of his stare made her uncomfortable.

"That's very good, Danny," she said, then winced slightly. She had meant to sound cheerful, but the words had come out overly hearty and even condescending.

Biting her lip, she mounted the horse and let him lead the way. Behind the stables were acres and acres of open field, and she relaxed slightly when she saw they were heading in that direction. Maybe if they rode fast enough she wouldn't have to make conversation.

For a while, she could feel him watching her, then as though he had assessed her ability, he gradually picked up the pace. Following his lead, she spurred her horse on. Soon they were racing across open country.

It felt good to be on a horse again, she thought suddenly. The wind in her hair, the feel of the powerful animal beneath her, brought an unexpected excitement to her blood. She was ready for this. It had been a tense day, and this was just the release she needed. Exhilarated, she laughed aloud as she bent forward and the scenery blurred softly.

They must have ridden several miles in a circuitous route before Danny slowed the pace then pulled his horse to a stop beside a wooded area. When he dismounted, Amanda, for a moment, simply sat in the saddle. Then feeling slightly foolish, she slung her leg over the saddle and slid down, tethering her horse beside his.

"I like it here," Danny said quietly as he moved a little way into the woods. "The gardeners never work here."

"It's nice," she said shortly, bending down to remove a piece of grass from the strap of her boot.

Suddenly Danny dropped to his knees beside a tree. Startled, Amanda glanced around. They were miles from Greenleigh. *Please,* she thought in panic, *please don't let him have a fit.* How did she get herself into these situations? She was simply not equipped to handle the mentally handicapped. Why didn't they make his keeper stay with him?

Danny turned around, cupping something in his hands. "Look," he said softly, a strange quality in his voice.

She glanced quickly, nervously at his hands, then away. Then slowly she looked back again. In his large hands he held a tiny blue flower. The contrast—delicacy cradled by strength—took her breath away. When she stepped closer, he handed it to her as though it were a great treasure.

"Look at its petals," he said softly. "It's like a...a..." He tensed as he seemed to struggle to find a word. "A miracle," he finished triumphantly.

Suddenly, unexplainably, she wanted to cry.

For a moment, he studied her face in silence. "Why don't you like me?" he asked quietly. "Is it because I'm one of the loonies?"

"Don't say that!" she snapped, her voice harsh. "Don't ever say that word again."

Rocking back on his heels, he examined her face in curiosity. "Miss Carey says it all the time."

"I don't care," she whispered tightly. "It's a cruel word."

"I've made you sad." The words were soft and slow, and there was deep regret in his voice, as though he were sad for her.

Amanda inhaled deeply, feeling again the unreasonable tears spring to her eyes. Then, awkwardly, she sank to sit beside him, staring at the flower in her hand.

After a moment, he said quietly. "Can I help?"

She gave a harsh laugh. "I don't think so. I don't like myself very much right now, Danny." She glanced away. "You see, I've just discovered I'm not a nice person—not nice at all." She met his eyes and her voice was husky when she spoke again. "I don't know how to deal with you. You're different, and that difference makes me uncomfortable." She leaned her head against the rough bark and said, her voice cutting, "And above all, Amanda must have her comfort."

He picked up her hand gently. "You're wrong, you know," he said quietly.

She glanced at him from the corners of her eyes. "How do you figure that?"

He stared at the sky, his strong face troubled. "I make you uncomfortable...but—" He broke off and squeezed his eyes shut in frustration. "But it *matters* to you." He snapped a stick between powerful fingers. "I wish I could say it right."

He had said it just exactly right, but she couldn't tell him so. There was too much emotion between them. It had to calm down or explode.

"I thought we were supposed to be riding," she said, her voice purposely light. "If I sit here much longer I'm going to take root."

"Then you would be a flower, and I would pick you," he said, laughing as he stood up. He took her hand to help her up, but his strength surprised them both, and as he gave her a jerk, she was pulled hard against his chest, knocking the breath from her.

"Danny," she said breathlessly, "finding a new friend is a wonderful thing, a special thing. It's an event I would like to stay conscious to appreciate. I won't do that if you keep knocking me senseless."

He laughed in delight, interpreting her mood if not her words.

"Seriously," she said, "you have to be very careful of your strength. It's normal to you, but others are not so strong."

A playful gleam appeared in his unusual gray eyes. "Danny," she said warily, "I don't like that look. What are you thinking?"

He grabbed her waist and held her up in the air. "I'm thinking that I like being strong," he said in satisfaction as he turned her sideways over his head so that she looked down at him.

"Daniel Phillips," she said, trying to make her voice stern, but it was hard to sound dignified when she was hanging in the air. "Put me down." Her lip quivered.

He smiled up at her. "Why?"

"Put me down," she said again, and this time the laughter in her voice was obvious.

"You look funny upside down," he said, cocking his head to one side to study her. "Like those faces people make on their fists."

"What a lovely compliment," she said, opening her eyes wide. "I bet you're known as the Byron of Greenleigh. Immortal words," she said, watching the laughter grow in his strong face. "Words to put on my tombstone. 'She had a face like one of those that people make on their fists.'"

Deep laughter rang through the trees as he sat down with her in his arms. She leaned against him, sharing the joy she felt in him. When he lay back, he pulled her along with him.

Then, as Amanda watched, his eyes turned green. It was the damnedest thing she had ever witnessed. One minute they were deep, placid gray; the next minute they were emerald green. Stunned, Amanda stared into them and found a blazing green fire...and she couldn't look away.

She was transported to another place in those eyes, to another time. He took her over completely until she felt she had lived a lifetime in those eyes, a lifetime in green fire.

Then the green faded and calm gray took over. The change left her weak. She felt lost as though something important had disappeared. Rolling away abruptly, she felt the color drain from her face.

"Why do you look funny?"

She swallowed heavily, plucking a blade of grass. "Funny, ha-ha?"

"No, like you found a worm in your apple."

Her laugh was hesitant. "I guess I'm not used to having a friend yet."

"It's nice, isn't it?"

She felt the tension drain from her. It was all right, she thought. She was comfortable again. "Yes," she murmured. "Yes, it's nice."

They lay on their backs, staring up at the clouds. "Where do you suppose the clouds will go from here?" Danny asked after a moment, his voice quiet. "Who do you think will see them next?"

"Oh, I don't know. Maybe they'll go to Hollywood to audition for a movie."

He laughed. "Not a monster movie," he said. "One with music. They're musical kind of clouds." He was silent for a moment. "They pass over us and then the highway, then what else will they see on their way to Hollywood? Tell me what they'll see, Mandy."

She smiled. She liked that. No one had ever called her Mandy. She had never thought she was a Mandy sort of person, but now, with Danny, she was.

"Oh, I don't know," she said lazily. "They might see traffic on the highway. Then maybe horse ranches and things growing. Maybe the people on the ranches are lying on their backs wondering where the clouds will go next."

"We could tell them." His voice was soft and husky. "They're on their way to Hollywood to be movie stars."

"I think they have to be parking-lot attendants first."

He gave a shout of surprised laughter. Rolling over, he leaned on one elbow to stare down at her. "It's nice

talking to you. No one else can—'' He frowned as
though reaching for a word that was just beyond his
grasp. "No one else can make dreams with me."

She reached up to touch his face. "That's important, isn't it? Having someone to make dreams with
you."

As she stared into his eyes something grew inside
her, something warm and comforting. *Why,* she
thought in amazement, *we really are friends.* She had
thought that she was merely humoring him. But that
was wrong. She felt a closeness, an empathy, that
didn't include an ounce of pity. Once she had passed
the barrier of her own making, she found that they
were curiously equal. They accepted each other as they
each were in reality. It was something rare that she had
found, something rare and fine and beyond her understanding.

During the two weeks that followed, the friendship
between Amanda and Danny grew. The brightest part
of her day was the time she spent with Danny. He was
the friend she had missed in the gypsy years of her
childhood. They played tennis and rode and walked
and swam. And they laughed. Always with Danny
there was laughter.

He had a way of making her look at the world dif-
ferently. He found something new and wonderful
around every corner. With Danny, there were miracles under their very feet.

Dr. Sutherland had left for England two days after
her arrival, but she hadn't missed him. In the past two

weeks she had gotten to know the others—guests and staff alike—who inhabited Greenleigh Acres.

Ginny had come to be a friend. Amanda now knew the harassed state she had found the nurse in that first day was chronic. She was obviously in love with Paul Choate, but just as obviously, something had gone wrong between them. Something Ginny refused to talk about.

Evelyn Baxter, the mischievous stripper, each day found a new way to liven the place up. Whenever Amanda heard a sudden shriek, a startled gasp, she knew that Evelyn was at work again.

Then there was Virgie DeVries. Virgie was no longer just an oddity to Amanda. She was brash and vulgar and harsh, but her sense of humor outshone all the other qualities. Always, beneath the brashness, beneath the sarcasm, Virgie's eyes were scared.

But none of the residents at Greenleigh touched Amanda like Danny did, she thought as she leaned back in her leather chair, staring at the clock on the mantel. It was almost time for her to meet him, a daily occurrence now. She hadn't realized it was becoming a habit until the habit was already established.

The door opened and a small, fidgety girl rushed in. "Here's the Wilson file," Maxi said, sliding to a stop in front of Amanda's desk. "I'm sorry I took so long getting it back to you, but the insurance papers somehow got thrown away and I had to go through all the trash looking for them."

Amanda smiled. Maxi did odd jobs for what was unofficially called Pencil Pusher's Row. She lost or misplaced something on the average of twice a day.

But everyone covered for her because she was Dr. Nabors's niece and because they all liked her.

"That's all right, Maxi," Amanda said. "I didn't need it anyway." She studied the flustered girl. "Is something wrong? You look worried."

Maxi pushed back her frizzy blond hair. "I think Leah's going to try and get me fired," she said, her lip quivering. "She exploded when I lost her schedule."

Amanda frowned. Leah was the fly in everyone's ointment. She was beautiful and intelligent, but held herself above everyone. Amanda had caught her in small cruelties that seemed to be perpetrated for their own sake.

"Don't worry about Leah," Amanda said. "If you left, she would have one less person to torment."

Amanda had intended to be sarcastic, but crazily, Maxi brightened. "You're right," the girl said. "The next gofer might stand up to her." She glanced at the clock and smiled. "It's time for Danny."

Amanda laughed. Greenleigh was like a small rural town. It didn't take long for everyone to know everyone else's business.

When Maxi left, Amanda walked out and closed the door to her office, her steps eager. As she rounded a corner she almost ran into Maribel Fortnoy and Virgie. The older woman cradled a battered doll in her arms and had her tongue stuck out to her chin as she beligerently faced Virgie.

A social comment no doubt, Amanda thought wryly. Maribel Fortnoy was definitely no shrinking violet; she was more of a spoiled brat.

"Hello, Maribel. Virgie," Amanda said as she drew near. "What's up?"

Maribel glanced at Amanda, her belligerence giving way to pathos. "Don't tell them where I am," she whispered. "They'll punish me. They always do. They think I'm worth nothing."

"They might be on to something," Virgie muttered.

"Virgie," Amanda said, her voice scolding. She reached out to comfort Maribel, but the older woman backed away. "They won't punish you, Maribel. They only want you to be comfortable. Don't you think you should let someone know where you are? They might be worried."

"I've been trying to tell her that," Virgie said, leaning against the wall as though the whole thing were annoying, "but she's nutty as a fruitcake. She thinks they'll send her to bed without supper."

Maribel nodded. "They will. They'll starve me until I rot. And they'll take Debbie away from me and she'll die without me." She smoothed back the doll's matted hair.

Just then, Ginny rounded the corner. Her hair was awry as usual and she panted with exertion. "Maribel, there you are. Guess what I have for you?"

"You're going to tie me down," Maribel said in resignation.

"Not today, dear. The cook made those special cookies you like so much."

"The ones with lemon icing?" Suddenly Maribel was a little girl who had been promised a treat, a treat that she knew she didn't deserve.

"That's right. Come on, let's get some."

"Evelyn can't have any," Maribel said as Ginny guided her away. "She's been bad. We could give her share to Debbie. And I won't sit next to Mr. Avery; he tries to look under Debbie's dress."

"Mr. Avery has tried that a few times with me, too," Virgie said.

Amanda laughed as Virgie walked away, but the encounter disturbed her. Maribel had Sutherland's Complex. Danny had Sutherland's Complex. How could the difference between them be so enormous? Maribel was a fractious, whining tattletale. Danny was open and loving in the extreme.

Sometimes it scared Amanda. His openness made him so vulnerable. She simply couldn't bear the thought of his being hurt.

On the open side of the employees' wing, the garden extended clear to the woods. It was on the edge of the woods that she had arranged to meet Danny. As she made her way through the tame, brightly colored bushes, a frown marred her features. She had never felt the weight of a friendship before. Relationships had always been casual things to Amanda. Only now was she finding it to be a responsibility as well as a joy.

Suddenly, she saw him waiting beside a bush. When he heard her footsteps, he turned and his face lit up. All the brightness in her world was contained in the smile that shaped his strong lips. Amanda was enveloped by it. She felt her pulse quicken when he extended his hands to her.

As she caught them both in hers, she heard him whisper, "Mandy."

Why should that single word bring tears to her eyes? she wondered. Inhaling slowly, she smiled. "Have I kept you waiting?"

"I don't mind. While I wait I can think about seeing you. It makes my time with you longer." He pulled at her hand. "Come and look. I found a nest. The eggs are gone, but...but come see how the bird made it."

He held the nest up for her to examine. "Isn't it beautiful?" he said, his voice soft and husky.

Amanda touched the small nest. The intricacy of it was amazing. "And I bet this didn't even come with instructions," she said.

He laughed as she knew he would. Together they began to walk through the woods until they came to a spot on the bank of a clear stream. The sun filtered through the trees in golden threads. Soft, curly ferns grew along the edges of the water, making it a setting for a fantasy. It was Amanda's favorite spot among all the beauties of Greenleigh.

"One day..." she said softly as she sat beneath a towering oak, her knees drawn to her chest. "One day a unicorn is going to peep out from behind those ferns." She leaned back against the rough bark and smiled. "He'll be a world-weary unicorn, his tail ragtag, his horn scarred from fighting eons of morally upright unicorns. And he won't particularly care for virgins or perfection. And he'll be just exactly right for you and me, Danny."

Amanda never knew how much Danny understood, but he always, as he did now, kept his eyes on her face while she talked, as though he would memorize each of her features, as though he could absorb what she was saying rather than hear it.

These times with Danny were the only times Amanda felt she could truly be herself, no pretenses, no excuses. There were invisible threads of understanding between them, threads that wound tighter and tighter each day.

The silence between them drew out and suddenly she stiffened, instantly alert. Something was wrong. She glanced up, her body tense, her breath held. Her gaze met green fire. She felt the power of it, pulling her in, taking away her will. It was inside her, around her, filling every corner of her mind and her body.

He knew, she thought dazedly. She read knowledge in that green gaze.

Moving closer, he knelt beside her. She held herself still as he reached out to gently stroke her face. "Like Nidhug curled up at the root of Yggdrasil," he murmured, his voice deep and husky.

Amanda felt dizzy. The words echoed in her brain, growing louder and louder. Rising to her knees, she grasped his shoulders tightly. *"What did you say?"* she rasped out. "Tell me again."

He shook his head as though coming out of a trance. Slowly, he smiled. "I don't remember." He sat down and glanced at her from the corners of his gray eyes. "Was it rude? You look funny."

She reached up to touch his face, her hand shaking. "Try to remember, Danny. I think it's important."

"Danny!"

At the shout, they both turned and watched Tom Dicks approaching. "You two look cozy," he said, smiling.

Amanda didn't like him. She hadn't thought of him one way or another until that moment, but now she knew she didn't like him. There was a look on his face that was just a shade too avid as he watched them. She stood and dusted her pants. "Did you want something?"

"It's time for Danny's appointment with Dr. Nabors." His gaze drifted slowly over her body. "He'll have to cut his playtime short today." He didn't move, but simply stood staring at her.

"Was there something else you wanted, Tom?" she asked sharply.

He smiled and shook his head slowly. "Not a thing...how about you? Was there something else you wanted?"

When she glanced away from the malicious humor in his eyes, he laughed aloud. "Come on, Danny boy. Time to go."

Amanda turned to Danny, her features softening. "I'll see you tomorrow, Danny."

He nodded, giving Amanda a look that was so wistful, it broke her heart. But without protest, he turned and began to walk away with Tom.

When they were out of sight, Amanda leaned against the tree, feeling curiously weak. Something was happening to her, she thought shakily. Something that she had never felt before. And suddenly she was scared. She felt drained and weak, powerless to stop the future.

It was much later when she asked herself why she should want the future stopped at all.

Chapter Four

God, give me strength."

The groaned words brought Amanda's head up sharply. Ginny was closing the door with one ample hip. Today the nurse looked even more frazzled than usual. Her pale hair was pulled loose from the ponytail in places, and there was a wide run in her green stockings.

She set one of the two cups of coffee she carried on the desk in front of Amanda. The other she cradled between the fingers of both hands as she sat on the couch.

Amanda didn't even try to hide her smile. "Has Mr. Avery been getting frisky again?"

"Among others." Ginny sighed heavily and leaned back. "Virgie just tried to get a game of strip poker going in the old-timers' wing."

Choking on the coffee, Amanda raised one slender brow in startled inquiry. "She must have put up quite a fight. You look terrible."

"Virgie? No, she went back to her room like a lamb. It was the old people who did this. They rioted when I told them there would be no party today." She rested her chin on her fist. "Why don't we get any nice, normal old people? If you've ever wanted to know where old perverts go, you can stop wondering. They all come here."

Amanda laughed. "You know you would hate working with ordinary people. These people won't wither away and die. Their personalities are too strong. But that means it's more difficult to take care of them."

"Easy for you to say," she grumbled, then stood. "I'm for a swim. How about you?"

Amanda shook her head. "I've got a couple of things to take care of. But I'll see you later."

Amanda's eyes were thoughtful as the door closed behind her friend. She wished there was something she could do to help Ginny and Paul. From bits and pieces each had told her and from what she had seen on her own, she knew Leah was the problem. Whatever had happened, Paul was obviously as deeply in love with Ginny as she was with him.

Shutting a large manila folder, she leaned back in her chair then glanced at her watch. It was almost time for her to close up shop. It was hard to believe she had been at Greenleigh a whole month.

She smiled as she thought of the ride she had taken earlier today with Danny. When they had stopped to walk through the woods, he had found a baby rabbit caught in a tangle of blackberry brambles. She could still see his big square hands, the fingers tender as he pulled the animal free and set it on its way.

Rubbing her chin reflectively, she considered the curious relationship that had developed between them. In her mind, he was no longer mentally handicapped. He was not a patient. He was simply Danny. And they were friends.

She frowned, remembering the change that came over him at times. It didn't happen often, sometimes coming and going with breathtaking swiftness, sometimes lingering long enough to pull her into a bewildering green spell.

The difference in his features at those times was striking, puzzling her. His eyes looked deeper set, not so wide open, the lines around them and his mouth becoming harsher. The pupils of the eyes seemed to be darker. And the eyes themselves were the strangest of all. They didn't sparkle gray; they blazed with a green inferno.

She had thought of it often, remembering the look, analyzing it. Gradually, a curious idea had come to her. It was like before and after Adam had tasted the fruit of the Tree of Knowledge.

She shook her head. The idea was as incomprehensible as the dreams that plagued her each night. God, those dreams, she thought restlessly. They were dreams that she could never remember afterward, visions that left her disturbed because she always awoke from them yearning for something she didn't understand.

Smiling wryly, she wondered if she just might land in B-North after all. Hearing a slight noise, she glanced up, her eyes widening when she saw Ted walk into her office.

"I didn't know you were back," she said with genuine pleasure in her voice.

He smiled, recognizing the welcome. "Just an hour ago. I can't stay. I've come to extend a dinner invitation that's long overdue...a small, belated welcome celebration in my apartment."

She smiled. "Thank you. I'd like that."

"Good. Tonight at eight," he said, giving her the benefit of his even teeth and charming smile before he closed the door after him.

Leaning back in the leather chair, she tapped a pencil against her chin, her eyes thoughtful. This was the opportunity she had been waiting for. Ted would know about Danny's condition. Maybe he could tell her about the strange things that happened when they were together.

Later that evening, after dressing with more than usual care, she arrived at Ted's apartment a few minutes before eight. Choosing her timing carefully, she waited until they had finished dinner and sat in the living room, drinking an after-dinner liqueur.

Glancing at him over the rim of her crystal glass, she said, "Ted, can you tell me what exactly is wrong with Danny—Daniel Phillips?"

He settled back against the couch, looking lean and elegant in his dinner jacket. "You certainly don't ask easy questions," he said, chuckling. "That's like asking how the universe was formed." He fell silent for a moment. "Everyone makes the analogy between the brain and the computer, as though the brain's billions of neurons were connected by electrical circuits. But the fact is, the brain is more like a chemical soup. The old gray matter doesn't have a set of plans; it's a self-developing system, and its patterns are determined to a certain extent by experience." He smiled. "It writes its own programs on the basis of the input it receives. In short, the brain is alive—a dynamic system."

She nodded, as though he had told her something she understood or even wanted to know. This had nothing to do with the man she met every day, laughed with every day, the man with green fire in his eyes.

Ted leaned toward her. "The problem for researchers is that although we know a great deal about the functional properties of nerve cells in many regions of the brain, we don't know how high-level functions—thought, perception, feelings, all the things that make us human—arise from these properties." He shook his head. "We will probably never know everything about the brain. It's like asking the finger to consider the finger. Some doors will automatically lock simply with the asking of the question. But it's possible that we will identify individual molecular abnormalities."

Amanda was beginning to seethe with frustration. This sounded like a speech he would give to a group of interested lay people. It was not in any way an answer to the question she had asked.

"But how does all this relate to Danny?" she asked stubbornly.

He smiled slightly, and Amanda tried very hard to squelch the feeling that she was being patronized. Extremely intelligent people gave off a superior attitude without even being conscious of it.

"It's the memory portion of Daniel's brain that has been affected. Scientists do know that certain neurotransmitters—the chemical messengers that stimulate the neuron and prepare the brain to receive information—are involved in memory. Acetylcholine, for example. We're on the right track, but most of us are working blindly, simply on instinct. For instance, the medication that Phillips and Fortnoy receive brings about a reaction that is not understood. We don't know why it works. It simply does. But every day we're getting closer to understanding it." Leaning back, he sipped at his drink. "I find it very exciting work."

She leaned forward. "Does this mean there could be a breakthrough soon? That Danny could be cured?"

When he laughed and shook his head, Amanda gritted her teeth. "When I say we're getting close, I'm speaking objectively."

"Try speaking subjectively," she suggested tightly.

"Twenty years, fifty, who knows. It could possibly come in my lifetime," he said doubtfully.

But too late for Danny, she thought, suddenly feeling tired. She stood. "It's getting late. Dinner was wonderful, but I think I'd better go now."

He frowned, but rose with her and followed her to the door. "I need to check on some things in the lab," he said after intercepting her questioning glance.

As they walked, she remained silent. Her mind was swimming with neurons and computers and chemical soup. This was not Danny, she told herself in protest. Danny was life and laughter and joy.

She didn't know how long the melody had been a part of her thoughts, but as they approached the music room it grew louder. Someone was playing one of the pianos, and playing it beautifully. It wasn't restful music; it was stormy and intense, almost disturbing in its urgency.

Amanda paused outside the door to listen. Slowly, as if she were being pulled forward, she pushed the door open and stepped inside.

Danny sat at the grand piano, his body caught up in the music as he hunched over the piano. His movements had a feverish quality. This wasn't simply a composition memorized and performed. This was emotion carried from deep within to his fingertips. This was an angry conversation with no hesitations, no struggling to find the right words.

She didn't move until the music ended. Then she slumped slightly, as though released from a spell. It startled her when Ted passed her and walked into the room.

"He's not supposed to be here," he said as though Danny were a mislaid glove. "Where in hell is Dicks?" Striding to a table against the wall, he picked up a telephone and punched the numbers emphatically.

Amanda hadn't taken her eyes off Danny. Now she moved closer to the piano. "That was beautiful, Danny. I didn't know you could play."

He simply stared at her, his eyes puzzled and hurt. "What are you doing with Dr. Sutherland?"

Why should she suddenly feel guilty? "We had dinner together. He's my boss, Danny. You knew that."

He glanced at Ted, then back to her. Amanda didn't understand. Danny liked everyone. Why had he taken a dislike to Ted, the one man who was helping him?

Tom Dicks hurried into the room, smoothing his hair as he walked. He was gruff when he spoke to Danny, who had pushed back the piano bench to stand. At the door, Danny paused and looked back at her, staring for a moment in silence. Then he followed Tom out of the room.

Amanda stared in confusion at the piano. "I can't believe he's hopeless," she whispered. "Not when he can play the piano like that." She glanced up to find Ted standing beside her. "And sometimes he says things that a child couldn't possibly know."

"Don't get too involved with the patients," Ted said, his voice harsh. "You'll only get hurt. You wanted the truth and I tried to soften it for you. The truth is, Phillips's brain damage is irreversible. The adult part has deteriorated—withered—and will not regenerate. It's simply not possible."

She winced. "But—"

"Amanda," he said, his voice softer, more sympathetic, "these things you hear Phillips saying that are out of character, they're simply echoes of the past, lingering pieces of what he was. And what you just witnessed in here is called the Savant Syndrome. You've heard of it. An idiot displaying brilliance in a single area.''

"Danny is not an idiot,'' Amanda said, her voice tight and hard.

"He might just as well be. Phillips is a very wealthy man. Do you think I'm the only one who has tested him?'' He sounded hurt. "Experts all over the country have looked at him and they've all reached the same conclusion. Just because I'm the one who put a name to Sutherland's Complex doesn't mean it's not recognized by others in the field.''

She shook her head. "I'm sorry, Ted. I wasn't questioning your ability. I just hate the finality of it. I hate that it has to be this way for him.''

"We all do.'' He smiled down at her. "But the fact is, nothing can be done for Phillips except the medication he is already receiving. It keeps him nonviolent and keeps the brain from deteriorating further. You can't even imagine what that would be like. It would be a steady progression backward for him.''

She shuddered. "Then I thank God you developed the medication.''

"So do I.'' He put his arm around her. "Amanda, I'm going to ask you not to discuss his condition with Phillips. He wouldn't understand it, but if by some small chance he did, it would disrupt his life and worry him. Don't give him ideas that he can someday be normal. It won't ever happen and he can live a happy life as he is.''

She could see the wisdom in that, so she nodded.

"You're tired," he said softly. "Why don't you go to bed now?" He smiled wistfully. "I didn't plan for the evening to be over so quickly, but I suppose it's best."

"Yes, I'm tired," she murmured, not even glancing at him as she left the room. She started walking toward her bedroom, but she couldn't get Danny's face out of her mind. He had looked so lost, so hurt. Turning abruptly, she went in the direction of the next wing.

Tom's room was next to Danny's. But the door was open, and the room was empty. Maybe he was still with Danny, she thought, frowning. Or maybe he was with Leah. She wondered just how good was the care he gave Danny. Danny would certainly never complain.

When she moved on to Danny's room, she found the door slightly ajar. No sound came from within. Could he be asleep already? She didn't want to disturb him. If he had already forgotten the incident, then so could she.

She had turned to leave when she heard a sound from his room. It was barely audible, merely a soft whisper, a slight rearranging of the silence. Placing her hand on the door, she pushed it open.

Moonlight filled the room, giving it a tarnished silver sheen. It cast shadows around the dark furniture, but seemed to spotlight the two people on the bed.

Danny lay on his back, the covers rumpled around him. The dark hair of the girl who kneeled beside him, touching him, hid his features.

Amanda felt white-hot emotion explode inside her. *"Virgie!"*

The girl jumped as if struck and scrambled off the bed, swinging around to face Amanda. She opened her mouth to speak, then snapped it shut.

"What are you doing here?" Amanda's voice was shaking with anger. "You— Go back to your room."

For a moment Virgie stared at her belligerently, her fists clenched. Then she raised her chin and walked out of the room without a word.

Amanda stood where she was, too furious to move, even to think. Slowly she drew in deep calming breaths. Moving across the room, she sat on the bed next to Danny. "Dan—" His name stuck hard in her throat. She swallowed and began again. "Danny, I want to tell you something, and I want you to listen carefully to me."

"I always listen to you."

She smiled stiffly. "Yes, I know you do. It's just that this is very important." She paused, meeting his gaze. "Danny, your body belongs to you—no one else. That sounds simple, but sometimes other people...people who think they are smarter than you might want to touch you without your permission. What I want you to know is that you don't have to let them. It's all right to say no. No one has the right to touch you unless you want them to."

He was silent for a moment. "Do you mean Leah, too?"

She closed her eyes weakly. God, what had they been doing to him? "I mean anyone," she said hoarsely. "Even the people in charge. Even Dr. Sutherland. Even me."

"I wouldn't mind if you touched me."

She reached out to stroke his strong face. "That's because we're friends. But even a friend isn't allowed to take advantage of personal rights. Do you understand?"

He nodded slowly. "Mandy?" The word was soft and puzzled.

"Yes?"

"Funny things happened when Virgie was touching me. It was...it was like what I feel when I'm with you only not the same." He closed his eyes, turning his head away from her. "I can't say it right."

"It doesn't matter, Danny. I understand."

He exhaled slowly. "You always understand. You and me, we're the same, aren't we? We laugh together and... and we think of the same things. Does it make you mad to be like a loonie?"

"I thought I told you not to say that anymore." She sighed. "No, it doesn't make me mad. If I could be like anyone in the world it would be you."

"But you're not exactly the same," he said, and now there was a smile in his voice. "You're softer than I am. And you're round here." He reached out and touched her breast.

Amanda didn't move. Don't react, she told herself. It's the innocent gesture of a child. The silence drew out and only when he withdrew his hand did she allow herself to look at him...then sucked in a sharp breath.

The eyes of the man next to her were blazing, blazing hot and green with ancient sensuality. She was not only confused by the change; she was obsessed by it. How could it be only an echo? It was fiery hot; it was real.

Suddenly, he reached out again and grasped her neck, pulling her toward him. His hold was rough, but she was too caught up in an emerald spell, too helpless to resist.

Amanda almost screamed when she felt his lips on hers. They were warm and strong and hungry—and she knew them. It was as though a missing piece of the puzzle was put back in place. He was a part of her. She recognized the rightness of it immediately, and the rightness consumed her.

Oh, God! she thought, stiffening in shock, a moan caught in her throat. This was the dream! This was what she had been yearning for each morning when she awoke.

Placing her hands on his chest, she pushed away and stared at him in confusion. He seemed to tower over her, his features fierce in the darkness. Then slowly he relaxed, his eyes settled to gray and he was Danny again.

Rising, she pushed her hair back with a shaking hand. "You'd better go to sleep now, Danny," she said, her throat painfully tight.

"I'm glad you came to see me," he said softly. "Good night, Mandy."

"Yes," she rasped out. "Good night, Danny."

She couldn't get out of the room fast enough and felt her knees give way as she pulled the door closed behind her and leaned back against it. She pressed a hand to her eyes, blocking the light, wishing futilely that she could block out what had just happened in the room behind her.

When her heart stopped pounding crazily, she lowered her hand to find Tom Dicks standing not two feet away from her, watching her with that awful, knowing smile.

Pulling herself together, she moved away from the door and brushed past him without a word.

Chapter Five

Amanda stood in the middle of her darkened bedroom in taut silence. Her hands were still shaking. She couldn't see them, but she could feel them. Or maybe it was her soul that she felt shake.

Swallowing an anguished sound, she began to pace back and forth in the dark. She had been so angry with Virgie. But how much of that anger had been directed at herself because—God forgive her—she had wanted to touch him, too?

Think logically, she told herself, running trembling fingers through her hair. Danny was an attractive man. It was natural that she should be physically drawn to him. She would have to be blind not to be. It was like seeing a Rodin sculpture or a fresco by Michelangelo. Those things were untouchable in the way

Danny was untouchable. One could admire and feel stirrings deep within, but the admiration and the stirrings were detached. They were separated from reality.

She sank to the bed. The logic hadn't done an ounce of good. She still felt a tight knot of guilt in her stomach. It was as though her very human emotions had touched something that was above all that. It was not a very comfortable experience, and for her own mental well-being, she knew she would have to stay away from him, at least until she came to grips with her own feelings.

The long night showed on Amanda's face the next morning as she walked around the grounds before breakfast. The haunted restlessness that had begun in Danny's room had stayed with her through the night and now nagged at her like the dull remnants of a migraine headache.

It was not going to be easy staying away from Danny, she thought wearily as she followed a narrow path to an almost too picturesque wooden footbridge. In the middle she stopped, staring at a small waterfall in the distance, a frown adding lines to the sides of her mouth.

It meant rearranging the life she had made for herself at Greenleigh. It meant rearranging her emotions. She had weekends off, but until now she hadn't felt the need to leave. Perhaps now was the time. She needed to get back to the real world.

Maybe she would call her friend Eric in Long Beach. She shook back her dark hair, thinking of the tall, blond lawyer she had dated occasionally in the past. He would probably do her a world of good, she thought, rubbing her temple. Eric was always fun to be with. He always—

Who the hell did she think she was kidding? she thought in frustration. She had no interest in seeing Eric again. She couldn't call up one ounce of enthusiasm. And that was what worried her.

Turning, she walked off the bridge and ran straight into Virgie. "Oh...hi," she said, feeling embarrassed as she backed up a step.

Virgie laughed harshly. "Don't worry," she said, raising a cigarette to draw on it deeply. "It's not catching."

Amanda couldn't pull up a flip reply. Shoving her hands into the pockets of her white jeans, she started to walk away. Then something in Virgie's eyes stopped her.

Turning slowly back to her, Amanda said, "Virgie, I'm sorry about last night." The girl's face grew harder. "No, I mean it. I was wrong. I had other things on my mind, and I took it out on you. I shouldn't have lost my temper. It was inexcusable."

Virgie didn't answer. She simply stood there, silently staring up at the sky as she exhaled a cloud of blue smoke. If her hand hadn't trembled slightly, Amanda would have thought her unaffected.

"I...I don't think Danny understood what was happening," Amanda said, unable to forget the slight tremble. "So don't worry about him." Raising her gaze from the ground, Amanda was startled to see the sheen of tears in the girl's eyes. "Truly, Virgie. He still thinks you're wonderful."

Virgie glanced away. "What do you expect from a loonie? What in hell does he know?" She met Amanda's eyes. "Don't you think I know what I am? Do you think I like it? Don't you know that I'm as sick of the word 'Nympho' as Danny is of 'Loonie'? Hell, I'm not even a nymphomaniac, but that doesn't make any difference to people who like labels." She threw down the cigarette and crushed it viciously with the heel of her boot. "It's a handy little word that people like to throw around. Nymphomania is a rare biological disorder. I'm an addict. I'm addicted to sex the way Peter is to drugs and the way some people are to alcohol."

She leaned against a tree and for a while was silent. When she began to speak, her voice had a curious dead quality.

"I can remember when I would do anything for a fix—*anything*. Men were like Popsicles. If one was good, then the whole box was better. I would scheme and lie and do anything to get it. Then when it was over I would look at the man beside me—God! some of them you wouldn't believe—and I would feel like throwing up. Then the black, sick emptiness would come back and fill me up. I would feel the weight of it in my chest and in my stomach. Then I would get out of bed and start planning where I could find the next man. Maybe the next one would keep it away a little longer." She closed her eyes tightly. "I thought I had it under control, but sometimes—" She broke off abruptly.

"Virgie," Amanda whispered hoarsely. "I had no idea. I'm so sorry. You must have been through hell."

"Yes, poor, poor little Virgie."

Both women swung around. Peter sat on the grass a few feet away from them. Unfolding, he stood agilely and dusted the grass from his jeans as he walked closer.

"You really like people feeling sorry for you, don't you?" he said, staring at Virgie as though she were a specimen in a jar. "Do you think you're the only one in the world who has done things they are ashamed of? Did you make the mistake of thinking I was in the polite circle of designer drugs... 'I'm doing Ecstasy and you're shirt is *so* blue'... is that what you thought? Well, it wasn't that way. I can tell you how every illegal drug will affect you. Believe me, none of them are nice. Your rap sounds tame compared to some of the stuff I've done and seen. You said you cheat and lie. Did you ever steal? From your own grandparents? Two old people who never hurt a soul in their lives." He laughed harshly. "Don't give me all this poor Virgie bull."

Virgie's face was mottled and unattractive in her anger. "Who in hell do you think you are?" she rasped out. "Did I ask for your pity? Did I even ask for your opinion? You can take your theories and shove them up your ass. When you're on drugs, you're physically addicted. You've got a nice comfortable safety net to fall back on. *You* didn't do it. The drugs did. Don't tell me I shouldn't feel the way I feel because you don't know anything about it."

"Feel all you want to feel," he said, throwing out an arm vehemently. "But at least admit that, problems notwithstanding, Virgie DeVries, deep down, is a nice person. *Allow* yourself to be nice, Virgie.''

She made a sound in her throat. Holding her gaze, he stepped closer to her. "Virgie, damn it, I don't care what your father has told you. His halo has slipped down on his fat head and is constricting his brain.''

She laughed, an abrupt, reluctant sound.

Peter smiled. "Forget him. Don't try to be hard. You can't be. It's against your nature.''

Again tears shone in her eyes. She turned away sharply. "You're beginning to sound just as preachy as him. Don't waste your time.'' Her voice broke on the last word and she strode quickly away.

Amanda watched as Peter caught up with her. She heard them shouting. Vile words poured out of Virgie, but Peter matched her word for word as though it were some kind of contest. When she tried to walk away from him again, he caught her arm, and suddenly Virgie was leaning against him, crying in harsh, ugly sobs.

Amanda walked slowly away. They didn't need intruders. She had the feeling that Virgie would be all right. And Peter, too. It was only slightly satisfying to know that something would turn out right.

Amanda didn't stop walking. She walked and walked, knowing that she had by now missed breakfast. After endless steps she came to another bridge, wider than the other to accommodate horses. Looking down at the small stream, she barely heard the sound it made as it ran over the rocks.

Suddenly, near the edge of the stream, she saw a stone, round and smooth and streaked with deep purple. Danny would like it, she thought, a smile tugging at her lips. He would think it was a miracle.

Shaking her head, she sighed. There was no way she could stop thinking about him. She walked off the bridge and scrambled down the steep slope. It couldn't hurt just to give him a rock, she told herself defensively.

Picking up the smooth stone, she shook the water off and slid it into her pocket, then sat beneath the bridge in the shadows. It was cool and peaceful beside the stream. Maybe here she could decide what to do.

She must have been half-asleep when she first heard the voices. She didn't hear individual words, just the murmur of voices in the distance. They they drew closer, and she heard the footsteps on the bridge above her. Whoever it was wouldn't be able to see her, she thought in relief. Virgie had been one encounter too many.

Pulling back into the shadows, she leaned her head against the wooden support.

"...been seven months, for God's sake. Isn't there any way to speed this thing up? You never told me it would last so long."

Amanda hated being put in the position of eavesdropper. But although she tried to tune out the words, the man's voice came to her clearly in her hiding place. He sounded nervous and irritated.

"You're wrong. I told you that in order for this to work you would have to turn the complete process over to me. You're too impatient. That's a mistake."

Amanda identified the second voice immediately. It was Ted's. He was speaking in that stilted, professional tone he used when discussing a patient. The other man was obviously worried about one of Greenleigh's guests, but Ted's words were not in the least sympathetic. Maybe the doctor's reputation eliminated the need for a winning bedside manner.

"If you don't trust me and my methods," Ted continued, "I can turn over the patient to you right now."

"You know damn well that's impossible." The stranger inhaled roughly. "Okay, maybe I'm pushing things. I know it's all worth it, but sometimes I wonder if it's ever going to work out."

"You came to me because I'm the best." Ted laughed softly. "Considering the money you're paying for this, I would think you would have a little more confidence in my work. If you have to concentrate on something, concentrate on what the future will be like when the treatment is complete. That should keep you busy for a while."

They were across the bridge now, and Amanda couldn't hear them so clearly. She was able to shut out the words, but from the rumble of voices, she knew when they turned from the bridle path and began to walk beside the stream. Amanda moved farther into the shadows. She saw the stranger clearly now and wondered which of the patients belonged to him. It was obviously one of the people in Danny's wing.

He was young and attractive with brown, curly hair. One curl hung slightly askew on his forehead. It looked artificial, as though someone had told him it gave him a cute, boyish look. But it was his eyebrows that were his most outstanding feature. They were heavy but curiously pale compared to his hair.

She frowned. There was something about him that struck a chord. She was almost sure she had seen him before. It always bothered her to recognize someone without being able to place him. He was probably on television, she decided finally. Greenleigh seemed to attract an inordinate number of people in show business. Maybe he was one of those enthusiastic used-car salesmen that one sees constantly on television but never pays attention to.

Suddenly the two men separated. Ted walked toward Greenleigh, but the stranger turned back toward the woods. Amanda couldn't think of anything in that direction, but decided he probably needed to walk and think, as she had.

When they were both out of sight, Amanda stood and climbed up the bank. Frowning slightly, it suddenly occurred to her that Danny never had visitors. Amanda had been at Greenleigh Acres for over a month, and not one person had been to see him in all that time.

Glancing at her watch, she caught her breath and quickened her steps. She was ten minutes late already. By the time she reached her office, Amanda was out of breath. She swung the door open, then stopped abruptly.

Ginny and Paul stood in the center of her office, their voices low, their faces contorted in anger. When they realized she was there, Paul swung past her and out the door.

"What happened?" Amanda asked quietly.

"Nothing. Absolutely nothing," Ginny said, her voice harsh. "Just the same old thing. If he would just tell the truth, then we could go on from there. But he keeps telling the same lie."

"About what?"

Ginny clenched her fists and walked to the window. "Amanda, I *saw* him kissing Leah. I didn't imagine it."

"Today?" Amanda asked in disbelief.

"No, two months ago. And he is trying to tell me that he didn't have anything to do with it." She laughed roughly. "He was a poor, innocent victim."

"Knowing Leah, I don't find that hard to believe," Amanda said dryly.

"Oh, sure. She forced herself on him." The nurse shook her head. "Hell, I knew it would happen sooner or later. He's handsome and intelligent and sensitive. What does he want with a loser like me? Fifteen pounds overweight and hair like something out of a Japanese horror movie. I just wish he hadn't made me think he loved me."

Amanda sat at her desk, considering her friend. Ginny had obviously set herself up. She had gone into the affair with Paul expecting it to fall apart. When she had seen him kissing Leah it had only confirmed what she already believed.

"Give me a break, Ginny," Amanda said, her voice heavy with sarcasm. When the nurse swung around, she said, "No, sit down and be quiet. You've got things that Leah could never have. But you're too busy feeling sorry for yourself to see it. You've got warmth and humanity. She has cold perfection. Men are just scalps to Leah. You said Paul was intelligent; well, he's too intelligent to fall for a phony."

Ginny moved closer, a bewildered look on her face. "Leah likes causing trouble," Amanda continued. She thought of the blonde touching Danny, and her features became grim. "I've a good mind to do something drastic to her pretty face next time I see her."

Sinking to the couch, Ginny said, "I want to believe him. But how can I? It's perfectly reasonable that he should be attracted to her."

"It's not. It's stupid. And you're stupid to let that woman come between you. Have you ever thought that you're reacting exactly the way she wants you to? Why give her that satisfaction?"

She could see Ginny's mind working, the gears turning slowly. "You're right," the nurse said at last. "I've seen her smirking. I don't think she even likes Paul all that much. She just didn't want me to have him. When Delores's friend came to visit yesterday, and I took him out to the pool, Leah watched me with that narrow-eyed stare that will make cold chills run down your back. She's just waiting for me to crack. By God, she won't see it."

Amanda chuckled. "That's the stuff." She was silent for a moment, a frown twisting her lips. "Speaking of visitors, Ginny, does Danny get many?"

"None," she said, shaking her head. "Not one in all the time he's been with—" Ginny broke off, her eyes widening in horror. "Danny!" she gasped. "I forgot his medication! Paul and I—"

Amanda didn't give her time to finish. Her heart began to pound, and she was on her feet before the nurse could pull herself together. Within seconds she was out the door with Ginny close behind.

They heard the shouts before they reached his room. When they rushed in, Tom Dicks and another man were trying to hold Danny down, trying and failing.

Amanda couldn't believe it. They had told her he would become violent, but it hadn't seemed possible. Not her Danny. Not her *parfait gentil* knight.

Ginny went immediately to the phone to call for help, leaving Amanda standing helplessly just inside the door. She couldn't stand to see him like this. She had to do something to help.

She moved toward him. "Danny, it's Mandy," she said, her voice soothing. "I'm here now. You're okay. Everything will be all right now."

"Don't get too close, Miss," the guard yelled.

But it was too late. Before either of the men could prevent it, Danny lashed out and struck her across the chest, knocking her back against the bed. She felt a sharp pain in her side as she fell in a heap to the floor.

At that moment three men rushed into the bedroom. The five men together held Danny down on the bed while Ginny gave him his injection. Amanda moved out of the way and watched it all in tense silence.

Almost immediately Danny subsided, his breathing hard, his eyes closed. Ginny spoke quietly to the guards. Then when all the men except Tom had gone, she turned to Amanda.

"Are you all right?" she asked.

Amanda nodded slowly. "I'm fine. It was stupid of me to think I could help him," she said, forcing her voice to sound calm.

But Amanda was anything but calm. She had lied to Ginny. She wasn't all right, and she didn't know if she would ever be all right again. When Danny struck out at her she had seen something in his eyes that she would never forget. She had seen a cold, deep fury, and unbelievably, she had seen terror.

Slowly she stood. As she drew near him, he turned his head. Suddenly a small smile twisted his strong lips. "Mandy," he said softly. "Your hair is mussed. I like it."

Amanda almost cried. Murmuring an excuse, she quickly left his room and made her way back to her office.

She was too involved with him, she told herself over and over again as she rocked back and forth in the leather chair. It had to change. And it had to change now. She couldn't take any more. Her nerves were stretched to the breaking point. If things continued the way they were, she would explode in sheer excess of emotion.

All morning she worked like a woman possessed, trying to keep her mind off him. But every few minutes, she glanced at the wall clock. Their usual time together came and went, and the minutes slowed.

Twenty minutes after she should have met Danny, the door to her office opened, and Ted walked in. Amanda put aside her pencil with a sigh. She found she liked the famous Dr. Sutherland less and less every day, but anything was better than being alone with her thoughts.

"I'm sorry our evening was cut short," he said, his smile showing just the right mixture of charm and regret.

Amanda glanced at him quizzically. She had thought their evening was over when they left his apartment.

"Of course people would have talked if you had stayed at my place." Sitting on the edge of her desk, he picked up her hand. "But there's a small room in the basement where no one would have found us."

Oh, great, she thought wearily. A lecherous boss was all she needed now. Why couldn't everyone leave her alone so that she could go quietly insane?

As she watched in reluctant fascination, he lifted her hand to his mouth. He didn't so much kiss it as wrap his lips around her knuckles. She had seen the look in his eyes before, and it had always spelled trouble.

Standing abruptly, she moved away from the desk. "I've never seen the basement. Ginny says your lab is really something."

"How would you like to see it tonight?" he asked, slowly stalking her.

"That would be nice, but I'm afraid I've made plans for tonight." Every step backward she took was matched by one forward from Ted.

This is ridiculous, she told herself as her back met the wall. It was something out of a French farce, and never had she been less in the mood for a farce.

"Don't you know why I hired you, Amanda?" he said softly, his fingers stroking her hair. "That first day I saw you, I could tell you were just as attracted to me as I was to you. It was unfortunate that I had to leave for England so soon after you arrived.''

He seemed to take it for granted that she was willing, Amanda thought, staring at him curiously. He was probably used to women jumping enthusiastically into his bed. Odds were he didn't even have to ask them.

But not Amanda. Never Amanda, she told herself in determination. It was an awkward position to be in. She couldn't bear to leave Greenleigh now. But as he pressed his lower body against her, she felt that the choice had been taken out of her hands.

Keep cool, she told herself, fighting the urge to kick him. There had to be a way out of this, a way that would let her keep her job and her virtue.

Suddenly, amazingly, Ted was jerked away from her. Blinking rapidly, she caught her breath in surprise. Danny was beside her, holding Ted by the scruff of the neck so that only the tips of his handmade Italian shoes touched the floor.

"You're late," Danny said calmly. "We were going for a walk."

Her lips twitched. "Yes, you're right," she said, the words choked. "We'll go right now. But first I'd like you to put Dr. Sutherland down—he's beginning to turn purple." She smiled up into Danny's peaceful eyes. "It clashes with his tie."

Danny slanted a look at Ted, then slowly lowered him to the floor. Taking Amanda's arm, he led the way to the door. Behind them, Amanda could hear Ted gasping for breath.

When they walked out a side door into the open air, she laughed, softly at first, then louder with exhilaration as they ran toward the woods. They didn't stop until they reached their spot by the stream. Then they threw themselves on the grass, catching their breath.

Danny glanced at her, smiling. "I like to hear you laugh. Maybe I should pick the doctor up every day."

"That's not a bad idea," she said, drawing in a calming breath. "No, I'm just teasing. You remember what I told you about your strength. It wasn't nice to make the doctor look like a fool." A bigger fool, she added silently.

Danny stared at the horizon. "I don't like him. He's..." He frowned and she knew he was trying to reach for a word, a thought. It hurt to see the frustration in his face.

It was so wrong, she thought. She simply refused to believe Danny couldn't be helped with therapy. She knew that Ted had told her, but doctors had been known to make mistakes. Danny was a special case. He was different. There was something below the surface that needed exploring, something...

Suddenly Amanda felt weak as the truth hit her like a tidal wave. She believed he was different because she wanted it to be so. Because she loved him. Not as she would love a child but as she could love a man.

My God! she thought weakly. It couldn't be happening. She had known she was too involved; she had known it for days. But the possibility that she could be falling in love with him had never occurred to her. Not even when she admitted she had never in her life been as happy as when she was with Danny.

She pushed her hands roughly through her dark hair. What was she going to do? What *could* she do? She needed to think.

"I wish—"

She glanced at Danny to find him staring at her, his gray eyes brooding. "What do you wish, Danny?"

"I wish it was all different."

"Different how?"

He shook his head. "I don't know. I wish I weren't me or you weren't you." He sat up abruptly. "I said we were alike, but we're not. You and Dr. Sutherland are alike."

He had said aloud what she had not been able to admit even to herself. There was a dividing wall between them. An insurmountable wall. Racial, social, religious barriers were nothing compared to the barrier between them.

He stood up and for a moment his eyes met hers, then he glanced away quickly. But not quickly enough. Amanda had seen and recognized the hopelessness in his eyes. It was the same hopelessness she felt in her heart.

"Oh, Danny," she whispered as she watched him walk away from her. "What are we going to do now?"

Chapter Six

It was only two days later that Amanda heard about Maribel Fortnoy.

As usual, Ginny had come in to spend her morning coffee break in Amanda's office. Amanda, preoccupied as she was with her relationship with Danny, only half listened to the nurse's bits of gossip. It took her a while to sense a restlessness in her friend.

"Is something bothering you?" she asked.

Ginny set down her cup. "Sometimes I don't know why I ever became a nurse. Why couldn't I have chosen something dull—like prostitution or bomb control? Anything would be better than this."

"You really are upset," Amanda said in surprise. "What's wrong?"

"Oh, I don't know," she said in exasperation. "I seem to be in a mood lately. Everything gets to me. Now we've been asked to double Maribel's medication, and it just seemed like the last straw."

Amanda glanced up from her coffee. The tone of Ginny's voice should have warned her, but it didn't. It simply sounded like nurse talk.

"I hate it when they get worse," Ginny said, pushing her hair back with a careless hand. "It's bad enough with a regular patient, but when it's one of the Special Ones, Dr. Sutherland takes it hard."

Now she had Amanda's complete attention. "What's wrong with Maribel? I didn't even know she was sick. When her niece was here yesterday, she looked fine." Amanda thought of the older woman as she had seen her the day before, all pink and white ruffles, a smear of chocolate on her chin. "I don't like her niece," Amanda added, frowning. "She was abrupt with Maribel. I know Maribel's a pain sometimes, but that's no excuse for rudeness."

Ginny nodded her agreement. "I didn't care much for her either, but that won't keep her from getting all of poor old Maribel's money when she dies." She gave Amanda a significant look. "The niece is her only relative."

"Is there a chance of that happening?" Amanda asked, shocked somehow at the thought of it.

Ginny shrugged. "She's not good. She's given all the nurses hell, but I hate to see her get sick. Dr. Sutherland ordered her medication doubled this morning...that's always a bad sign." She sighed. "That poor man. He gets involved with all his patients. But especially the ones with Sutherland's Complex.''

Amanda had seen no evidence of that herself. In fact, beneath the surface, he seemed to be a rather cold man. But it wasn't Amanda's place to burst Ginny's bubble.

"He takes it as a personal failure when something happens to them because it's his specialty," Ginny continued.

"Well," Amanda said as she picked up her coffee cup, "let's just hope she gets better."

But she didn't. The next morning, the word went around in whispers as though it were a mysterious disease that would somehow spread if spoken of aloud—Maribel was failing.

During her morning break Amanda made her way to B-North to see Maribel for herself. She walked into the older woman's room, nodding to the nurse who sat beside the bed. The room was dim, but there was enough light for her to see that the whispers had been true. The woman on the bed was an empty shell. She looked directly at Amanda, but there was no recognition in her pale eyes.

"Maribel?" Amanda said softly.

"She won't know you," the nurse said, her voice subdued. "She's already gone past that. Last night she lost control of her movements and her bodily functions. I'm afraid she hasn't got long."

How could it happen so fast? Amanda wondered, rubbing her temple as she turned to leave the room. Dying shouldn't happen this quickly if it wasn't through violence. Disease should linger and give one time to get used to it.

She couldn't get Maribel out of her mind, even when she met Danny at the stables. As though sensing her mood, he set a frantic pace. They rode hard and fast, and at times she felt they were trying to outrun fate.

By the time they dismounted beside the woods, Amanda felt less restless, but it was only as they walked through the woods that she actually felt peace return.

"Do you ever get scared?" Danny asked suddenly.

"All the time, Danny," she said quietly. "All the time." She glanced at him in concern. "Why do you ask? Has something scared you?"

"It isn't something exactly. Sometimes... not any special time, just sometimes, I feel funny. Dizzy or something—I can't explain—and... and I know something is wrong, and I can't tell what it is." He glanced at her. "They said Mrs. Fortnoy is dying."

"And hearing that made you feel the strange way?"

"Not exactly. It just makes me remember those times. And I don't want to remember them. I want to pretend they never happen."

"Come on, let's sit down." They walked down a slope toward a pond and lay propped up on their elbows as they watched the ducks.

"My father used to tell me a story," she said, smiling as she sat up and wrapped her arms around her legs. "I remember the first time he told it—I must have been about five at the time—and in the middle of the night I woke up from a nightmare with my heart pounding like it wanted to get out of my chest. I ran down the hall to my parents' bedroom." She laughed. "Oh, how I begged to sleep with them. Just this one time, I said. But my father wouldn't let me. He sat on the side of the bed with me on his lap, and he made me tell him all about the dream. It was full of shadows and robbers and dragons that especially like to eat five-year-old girls."

Danny smiled slightly, his eyes trained on her face as she continued. "When I finished, he told me a story about a little girl who was afraid. Not just of dragons but of everything. She hid in a box because inside she felt safe; she had definite boundaries, and she could see into every corner. Nothing could get her there." She glanced at Danny. "At the age of five that didn't sound so bad. But then he started to tell me what else couldn't get into the box. Things like laughter and sunshine and love. Nothing new and exciting could happen because nothing could get in. Then he told me something I'll never forget. He said, 'Amanda, nothing in the world is as bad as being afraid—no dragons, no monsters, no shadows. You've got to turn on what frightens you. That way you control the fear instead of letting it control you. Confront the dragon, baby. Always confront the dragon.'"

She picked up Danny's hand. "I've been afraid a lot of times since then, Danny. But I always remember what he told me. I've found out that fear is a diminishing emotion. It makes you seem less in your own eyes. So let's make a pact. When either one of us gets scared we'll find the other, and we'll confront the dragon together."

He stared down at her silently for a long time, then he said, "I love you so much, Mandy."

Her breath caught in her throat. "I love you too, Danny," she whispered hoarsely.

Later that same afternoon, Amanda heard that Maribel Fortnoy was dead. She had known since her visit that it would come, but still it was a shock. She had never felt this particular helplessness, the frustration that death brought to the survivors. It left her restless. Dinner was out of the question, and she couldn't stand the thought of going to her room.

Maribel's file would have to be closed sooner or later, she thought as she shifted in the leather chair behind her desk. And there were insurance papers to be taken care of. Now was as good a time as any to tackle it all.

But when she went to the file cabinet and began going through the files, Maribel's was not among them. Muttering in annoyance, Amanda went to the nurses' station.

"Ginny," she called as she saw the nurse leaving. "I can't find Maribel's file. Was it kept somewhere else?"

"Not the financial records," Ginny said, frowning. "Her medical file is in the basement along with the other Special Ones. Dr. Sutherland keeps them there so that when he's working in the lab, he can pull them and compare them to his notes. The financial records are supposed to be in your office." She grimaced. "Lord, I hope Maxi hasn't screwed up again. If she stuck financial records in with the medical file, it could be the last straw."

Amanda shook her head. "There's no need for anyone to know. I'll simply go to the lab and check."

Ginny leaned against the wall, scratching her chin thoughtfully. "I'm afraid you can't do that. The laboratory and the file cabinet are both kept locked. Danny's and Maribel's medical records are always filed at the end of the day by Oates, the warden. Other than Dr. Sutherland, she's the only one who has the keys."

"But wouldn't she have noticed if a financial file was in there also?" Amanda asked.

"Are you kidding?" Ginny gave her a skeptical glance. "She only knows how to run this place. She would think it was beneath her to know about the files. She only takes care of them because it shows her authority—the Keeper of the Keys."

"All the files should be color-coded to keep mistakes like this from happening," Amanda said as she rubbed the back of her aching neck. "But I'm afraid that won't help Maxi right now. What a mess."

"Look," Ginny said, glancing around furtively, "I know where Oates keeps the keys. If you'll meet me in the basement, we can check the files and straighten them out without anyone knowing about it."

Amanda agreed readily, and later she arrived at the lab door just ahead of Ginny. "Thank goodness the warden was having her tea," Ginny said, unlocking the door. She handed Amanda the keys as they walked inside. "It's the small one. I'm going to check on a couple of the animals."

Ted's laboratory, covering the entire basement, was just as enormous, just as elaborate as Ginny had said.

Baffling machines and gadgets sat around on gleaming white counters. Along one wall was a row of cages containing, from what Amanda could see, monkeys and white rats.

The file cabinet was in one corner of the huge room, along with a small metal desk. Walking to the cabinet, Amanda unlocked it, feeling like a cat burglar as she began to go through the files.

"Egan...Everett...Falcon," she murmured, laying the keys on the top as she came to the right file. "Fortnoy."

She began to pull it out, but it was wedged up against the others and two more came with it. At that moment one of the monkeys screeched, causing her to jump skittishly. All three files fell to the floor.

"Oh, great," she muttered to herself. "Some great burglar you'd make."

Kneeling, she gathered up the papers, glancing through them to make sure they went back into the right folders. Suddenly her eye caught something in one of the files. Frowning, she looked at the other one and checked it also.

Standing abruptly, the papers she had held fell unheeded to the floor as she began going through the files in the cabinet. Her movements were awkward, becoming frantic as she checked file after file.

Suddenly she stopped and leaned against the cold metal cabinet. Her face was gray as she stood there trying to still the tremors that shook her from within.

Turning slowly, she walked toward Ginny, her movements stiff and mechanical. Ginny turned with a smile that died suddenly as she stared at Amanda. "What's wrong?"

Amanda closed her eyes and swallowed. "All those patients...those are the ones with Sutherland's Complex, is that right?"

Ginny nodded, her expression puzzled.

"There must be twenty, twenty-five files there, covering a seven-year period."

"Yes."

"Ginny...they all died," she whispered hoarsely. "Every one of them died."

Ginny sank back against the counter. "God, Amanda, I thought you knew. I'm sorry."

"Tell me."

"The Special Ones all die within two to two and a half years of developing the first symptoms. It would be a lot quicker if Dr. Sutherland hadn't discovered the drug we give them. What happened to Maribel would happen within weeks if left on its own."

It was too much. The room swam crazily around her; gravity pulled at her. She pressed a hand to her mouth, trying to remain upright.

Danny was going to die.

Chapter Seven

Amanda held on to the spotless white laboratory counter, trying to get the feel of something solid. *Don't let me scream,* she begged silently against the pain in her chest.

"Amanda?" Ginny was staring at her curiously. "I asked if you found the file."

Amanda shook her head. "No," she said, her voice sounding rough to her own ears. "No, it wasn't there."

She turned and walked out. In her room, she lay on the bed, staring up at the ceiling. The whole thing had a feeling of fantasy about it. It couldn't be happening. Danny was so young and strong. He simply couldn't be dying.

"God!" she cried aloud. The word was an exhortation; it was an angry plea, a shaken fist. But there was a wall of glass between her and God. She knew he was there, but she couldn't reach him. So she lay alone through the long night, falling into a restless sleep only when the first lifting of the darkness was visible through the window.

When she awoke, the weight of her discovery made her weary before she had even begun the day. She went through her work in a daze. When it was time to meet Danny, Amanda pushed back her chair with mechanical movements and walked out of Greenleigh toward the edge of the woods.

She saw him long before he saw her and couldn't take her eyes off him. She watched him, loving him, and today the loving had an acute feel to it, a painful, sharp edge.

"You're sad," he said in his soft, deep voice, his eyes sad for her as he watched her approach.

She felt tears surface and looked away, avoiding his caring gaze. "There are some days when you just wake up sad." She glanced at him to find him nodding in understanding. "I always tell myself that those sad days are mourning days. Days that we feel all the suffering in the world. We don't realize it, but since we're all a part of man, we have to share the pain sometimes."

"That makes it more important, doesn't it? I like the way you say it. That means... It's like..." She could see his hands clench into fists as he fought the hesitation. "You feel sad for no reason, or sad just because no one will even let you choose what shirt you want to put on." He exhaled and shook his head. "I can't say it right."

"No, I know what you mean. You said it just fine." She bit her lip. He felt guilty because he minded that the people here had taken away his freedom of choice, his dignity as a human being. Amanda felt the sadness slip away, and a welcome rush of anger took its place. Even though his surroundings were plush and his every need attended to, Danny had been dehumanized. The whole thing stank.

They began to walk, and today she steered him away from the place by the stream. She didn't think she could stand it. Not now, not so soon.

On the trail, they ran into John and stopped to talk. After a moment, Danny moved away to watch a group of noisy birds. Amanda stared after him, barely hearing what the old man beside her was saying.

"What's wrong, Amanda?" John said, breaking a silence she hadn't realized had fallen.

She turned back to look at him, her eyes stormy. "He's going to *die*," she said, the words erupting angrily as though they had been just below the surface. "I just found out, and it hurts so bad, John. I know it's wrong, but I feel like he's going to die a prisoner."

"It's not wrong," he said, staring after Danny. "Danny and I have both been left here to die. People don't like death, even the nicest people. They hide it away so they won't have to look at it. They don't want to be reminded that someday it will happen to them, too." He stooped to pick a weed. "I've had enough. I thought I could stand it to make my daughter feel better, but I can't. She's young. She'll have to work out her problems, her guilt on her own.''

He paused and glanced up at the blue sky. ''I'm leaving here. I'm going to find a place where I can participate in life again. If I could, I'd take Danny with me. We both need out of this velvet zoo.''

She stared at John for a moment, then put her arms around him. ''Good luck, John J. Pike.''

Danny came back as John walked away. ''Why were you hugging John J. Pike?''

''He's going to live somewhere else,'' she said. ''Somewhere where there are no gourmet meals, no designer drapes—and no walls.''

She wished it could be the same for Danny. She wished they could go somewhere where he could be free. Free to die with dignity.

Several days later, a thought came to her in the middle of a sleepless night. Why not? the voice said slyly. Why shouldn't she take Danny away and make what was left of his life happy?

No! I couldn't, she argued. It was wrong, legally and ethically wrong. But no matter how many times she said no, the thought persisted. And what of morality? the voice inside her asked. Shouldn't moral rights at times take precedence over legal and ethical rights?

Amanda couldn't say when she finally made the decision to take Danny away. It could have come as she watched him from day to day, feeling helpless to stop what was happening to him, for he had become an obsession, claiming all her thoughts, all her emotions. Or it could have come in the middle of one of her endless nights.

At first, she merely began asking questions about his care, then somehow she knew it wasn't only curiosity that prompted the questions. She was really going to do it.

It was two weeks later, as she lay on her bed staring at the ceiling, that she began to make definite plans. Greenleigh had always seemed a glamorous hideaway to Amanda. But suddenly it felt like a prison. The high walls that before had symbolized security and privacy now seemed ominous obstructions to their freedom. She could no longer regard Tom Dicks as a male nurse or a valet; as far as she was concerned he was a guard. Every entrance was watched, surreptitiously, by one of the men inside Greenleigh. Scads of gardeners moved around the grounds; surely no place needed so many gardeners.

The stone wall, the iron gate, the guards—why had she never seen the prison fixtures before? Through a casual conversation with Ginny, Amanda knew that it wasn't possible to take Danny for an outing away from Greenleigh. She would have to find a way around the security.

She rolled restlessly on the bed. Even if she managed to get him out, once they were away, then what? Where would they go? What would they do? What if the authorities found them and took Danny away from her?

She opened her eyes in the dark. She would simply have to marry him.

The idea rippled through her, shocking her, but she shoved aside the automatic reaction. If she was to have legal charge of him, it was necessary that they marry. They could go to Las Vegas; no one would even notice them there. Then to the mountains—to the cabin her parents had given her two years ago when they had moved to Ireland. She and Danny would be safe there, she told herself. And most important, Danny would be free.

Suddenly she caught her breath sharply. The medication! How could she have forgotten it? It was the most important thing. Danny's life depended on that drug.

It had all been for nothing, she told herself in despair. She felt all her plans slide away from her. Tears rolled helplessly down her cheeks as she clenched her fists and pounded the bed beside her.

"No!" she said aloud. She wouldn't accept defeat so easily. She couldn't. She had to find a way. She couldn't let Danny down. She would—

Suddenly, she lay perfectly still. She would simply steal the drug.

The idea came so easily, as though she made a habit of stealing. She almost laughed aloud. Amanda didn't even know herself anymore. But it didn't matter. Nothing mattered except Danny.

She would steal enough of the drug to last three months. Then she would come back for more. By that time there would be no doubt about the validity of their marriage.

But first, she thought, sliding down in the bed and hugging a pillow to her, she would have to learn how to give him his injections. Everything had to be exactly right before she made a move.

For days, in the privacy of her room, she practiced giving injections to an orange. She had given shots before to her diabetic cousin, but that had been years ago. She couldn't take any chances with Danny. They would be alone, and his life would depend on her.

"I tell you, Amanda, it's unbelievable. She looks me straight in the eye and then starts running her hands down his arm. And Paul," Ginny said in disgust. "Why doesn't he stop her? He just sits there like he's afraid to say anything."

Amanda glanced at Ginny as they walked down the hall together. "Some people are naturally shy of making scenes, Ginny. Besides, Leah is so sneaky about it; Paul would feel silly telling her to take her hands off him."

"Well, I wouldn't feel silly." She sighed, stopping in front of Danny's door. "What makes me furious is that we were beginning to talk again. I was beginning to think things might work out this time."

She reached out for the doorknob, then pulled back, holding out her hands. "Would you look at them," she said, staring at her trembling hands. "Why do I let her make me so furious? How am I going to give Danny his injection?"

Amanda felt her knees give way slightly. It was the chance she had been waiting for. Please, she begged silently, don't let me mess it up.

"Why don't you let me give it to him?" she said, her voice carefully casual.

Ginny glanced at her in surprise. "You? Have you done this before?"

"Hundreds of times," Amanda assured her, mentally crossing her fingers. "I have a diabetic cousin," she said, adding truth to strengthen the lie. "This is not all that different, is it?"

"No," Ginny said hesitantly. "They're both given in the muscle rather than the vein." Suddenly she shrugged. "Why not? You couldn't do any worse than I would with these hands, and Danny trusts you."

Yes, Danny trusted her. She just hoped that she deserved his trust.

When they entered the room, Danny was sitting on the bed. He wasn't doing anything; he was just sitting. When she saw the unreasonable joy that came into his eyes when he saw her, anger at his neglect gave her strength.

Under Ginny's supervision, she drew out the correct dosage, willing her hands to be steady. Then under Danny's trusting eyes, she administered the injection to his arm.

"That was perfect," Ginny said, unaware that she had just given Amanda and Danny their signal to freedom.

It was a week later, when she had made all her plans, when she had already asked for an emergency leave of absence to tend a sick aunt, that she first spoke to Danny.

She had put it off as long as she could, wondering how to phrase it, wondering how to convey the importance of silence to him. When they reached their spot by the stream, she said hesitantly, "Danny, how would you like it if the two of us left Greenleigh?"

His head jerked toward her, his eyes alert as he stared at her. "Leave here?" he asked, "like John J. Pike? Go somewhere, just the two of us and live together... without Tom Dicks?"

"Yes."

He closed his eyes tightly and inhaled a deep, slow breath. Then he opened them again and she could see the hopelessness there. "They wouldn't let us," he said, his voice tired. "I've tried to leave before, but they always stop me."

No one had told her he had tried to leave. But then no one would. Greenleigh must never seem less than wonderful. No wonder he was watched so carefully.

"I have a plan, Danny. No one would know but us. We would have to sneak away. Would you mind sneaking out?"

"I wouldn't mind anything if we can go someplace together." He stared up at the sky. "If we were away from everyone... if no one knew us, it wouldn't matter that we're different."

Please, let him be right, she begged silently.

Chapter Eight

Everyone knew Tom Dicks visited Leah at ten-thirty every night. "You can set your watch by it," they would say, sometimes in annoyance, sometimes with a suggestive grin. At ten he made sure his charge got dressed for bed, then he turned out Danny's light and sat in his own room thumbing through a girlie magazine until ten twenty-five. At ten-thirty he entered Leah's room without knocking. At exactly eleven twenty-five he left Leah's room, crossed to Danny's wing, opened the door of the darkened room to make sure Danny was still in bed. And at midnight every night Tom Dicks went to bed.

On this particular night, as Amanda sat in the darkness of her bedroom with two suitcases beside her on the floor—one an empty nylon carryall stuffed with newspaper—she was extremely grateful for the fact that Tom Dicks was a creature of habit.

Every second that passed seemed like an hour. It had all gone too smoothly; something had to happen. She had been so busy taking care of all the details, she hadn't had time until now to be afraid. But now she was very definitely afraid.

Confront the dragon, she told herself as she shifted restlessly on the hard chair. Mentally she ticked off all the things she had done in preparation. She knew exactly where each guard was posted, inside and out. Just minutes before, she had placed the call that gave her the excuse to leave tonight. Oates had been there when she made the call. She was very sympathetic when Amanda told her that Aunt Eddie had taken a turn for the worse. The housekeeper had agreed that Amanda would have to leave tonight.

Amanda stood and began to pace. The waiting was the worst. A thousand unoccupied seconds in which doubts could grow. She couldn't allow it. She had come too far, and her goal was too important.

"Think," she said aloud. Had she taken care of everything? Ralph had already brought her car around. It was waiting at the front door. And the key to the drug room—

She caught her breath, searching frantically in her pocket for the key. At last it slid into her fingers and she clutched it tightly, going weak with relief. Oates wouldn't notice it was missing for days. She kept it only because she held all the keys.

Amanda glanced at her watch. Ten forty-five. The nurse on duty would be starting her rounds now. It was finally time. Picking up her bags, she walked to the door, shifting them as she opened the door...to find Ginny, her hand raised to knock.

"Amanda—" she began, then glanced at the suitcases. "What are you doing? I thought you weren't leaving until tomorrow."

Amanda felt her hands tremble and clutched the handles of the bags tighter. She could feel the key to the drug room biting into her palm.

"I was," she said. "But when I called the hospital tonight to check on Aunt Eddie, they said she had had another spell, a bad one. So—well, I wouldn't feel right if I didn't try to get there tonight."

When had she gotten so adept at lying? she wondered as she allowed herself to glance at Ginny's face. There was not a hint of suspicion there. But why would there be? No one in their right mind would think of doing what Amanda was doing.

"I'm so sorry," Ginny said in genuine sympathy. "Here, let me carry one of your bags." She reached out for the empty carryall.

"No!" When Ginny gave her a quizzical look, Amanda said, "Don't bother, Ginny. I'm not going straight to the car. I promised Danny I would stop by to see him before I leave."

"Well...okay, but I wouldn't mind waiting."

"That's too much trouble. The bags aren't heavy." At least, one wasn't, she amended silently. Then she frowned. "Why did you come to my room? Did you need something?"

The nurse shook her head. "No, I was just restless. I thought maybe we could play cards or something."

"I would have liked that," Amanda said. "But as you see, I don't have time."

"I guess now is when I start that nine-pound Michener novel," Ginny said, turning away. "Drive carefully. And don't stay too long."

Amanda stood watching her walk away. "Ginny," she said hesitantly. When the nurse paused to glance back, Amanda swallowed heavily and said, "Thanks."

Ginny smiled. "For what?"

"I don't know... I guess for being a real friend."

Ginny nodded, then walked into her bedroom, closing the door behind her.

It was only when the fact that she had actually gotten through the first unexpected hazard sank in that Amanda began to shake. Lowering one suitcase to the floor, she pressed a hand to her mouth to hold back hysteria. "It will be all right," she whispered. "It'll be fine."

Drawing in a deep, bracing breath, she picked up the suitcase and walked down the hall.

There were two nurses' stations in Greenleigh, one in A-North for the old-timers and one in B-North—Danny's wing. Anyone entering or leaving either wing had to pass an open station, and at the back of each station was a small drug room.

As Amanda reached the top of the staircase that led to B-North, she spared a prayer of thanks that Ginny was not working tonight. Responsibility for the theft of the drug would fall on the nurse on duty. Not that that would have stopped Amanda. She had developed a hardness where Danny was concerned. Nothing was as important as making the rest of his life happy.

Keep that thought, she told herself. Keep thinking about what it's all about. Keep—

She stopped abruptly, feeling her knees buckle. There was a nurse behind the white counter. *She can't be here,* Amanda thought frantically. She simply couldn't be there.

But she was. It was Diana, the tall redhead who had informed Ginny of Mrs. Baxter's striptease that first day. Now Diana was staring at her inquisitively.

"Amanda," she said in surprise. "What are you doing up here?"

Stay calm. Drawing in a deep breath, she walked forward. "I have to leave tonight instead of tomorrow," she said. "I promised Danny I wouldn't leave without saying goodbye."

The nurse looked doubtful. "He's probably already asleep."

"Couldn't I just peek in?" Amanda asked. "I wouldn't disturb him. If he's already asleep, I'll just call him tomorrow from Los Angeles."

"Well . . . yes, I guess that would be all right."

"Thanks, Diana." She placed her bags in front of the counter. "Should I check with you when I leave?" she asked hesitantly.

Diana shook her head. "I'll be making my rounds in a second. I'll probably catch up with you."

Not if I can help it, Amanda thought as she walked away. The hall seemed a mile long, and as she reached Danny's room, she paused a get a grip on herself. Then she turned the handle and went in.

The room was dark. She moved inside, then stopped when she saw the shape in the bed. He couldn't have forgotten.

"Danny?" she said softly.

"Mandy." The voice came from directly behind her, and she almost fainted.

"Oh, Danny, you scared ten years off me," she whispered, relief making her weak. "What did you do to the bed?"

"I put pillows under the cover so Tom Dicks will think it's me."

"That's wonderful," she said, hugging him. "You make a perfect spy."

It was perfect. When Tom stopped by to check on his patient, he would think Danny was still in bed.

Danny held up a small leather bag. "I'm ready."

She pushed her hair back with a trembling hand. "We still have to get your medication," she murmured, more to herself than to Danny. "I thought she would be gone already. I wanted to have it all done by the time I came for you."

"I'll help you. It will be easier if I help."

She smiled. "Sure it will." She inhaled deeply. "Okay, here goes."

Walking to the door, she opened it and peeked out. No one was in the hall. Had the nurse already begun her rounds? At that moment, Diana stepped into the hall and closed a door behind her.

Amanda ducked back into Danny's room, holding her breath. She counted to ten, then opening the door a crack, she saw Diana enter the next room. She reached back and grabbed Danny's hand. "It's time," she whispered.

Together, they ran the length of the hall. When they reached the nurses' station, she grabbed the empty carryall, and the two of them moved around the counter to the door at the back of the small cubicle.

She still had the key in her hand, but now it was slick with her perspiration. She fumbled trying to insert it into the lock. It wouldn't go in. She couldn't make it go in.

"Let me," he said, taking the key from her.

His face was calm as he inserted it without a problem. It was then that Amanda finally realized they were in this thing together. It was as important to Danny as it was to her. Seconds later the door swung open.

The drug room was merely an outsize closet, but wooden shelves covered every available inch. Amanda quickly studied the labels on the shelves until she came to the one she was looking for.

Dumping the newspaper out of the nylon bag, she placed the bag on the floor and began to grab the boxes she knew contained vials of Danny's medication. In her haste, she brushed against a row of tall bottles, and the noise sounded thunderous in the small room.

"Shhh," Danny said behind her.

Amanda stifled a hysterical laugh. Somehow she felt she had been demoted to assistant. Over her shoulder she whispered, "We need two boxes of disposable syringes. I think they're on the shelf over there."

Danny opened several boxes before he found the right one, and by the time he had placed the syringes in the bag, Amanda had finished her own task. She didn't even try to lock the door as they left; Danny took care of it.

Once more she checked to make sure the hall was clear, then grabbed the large suitcase from in front of the counter, and walking side by side, they moved silently around the corner to the staircase.

They were going to make it, she kept telling herself. They were really going to make it.

The lounge, empty of guests, seemed enormous as she pushed open the door leading into it. It was like standing on a mountain, surveying a vast desert. There was no help for it; it had to be crossed.

They were so vulnerable here, she thought, so exposed. With every step she was sure someone would walk in and stop them. The deep carpeting muffled their steps, but to her own ears, even her breathing sounded loud.

They skirted the edge silently, knowing the guard could appear at any moment, knowing that he would spot them at once if he did.

They were only yards away from the front door when Amanda heard the footsteps. At first she thought it was the pounding of her own heart, but her heartbeat had never echoed.

She froze at the same moment she felt Danny grip her arm in warning. It was long seconds before she realized the footsteps weren't coming from the lounge, but from a carpetless hall or room nearby.

Silently motioning Danny to stand against the wall behind a tall Boule cabinet, she took the suitcase from him and waited for the guard to appear.

A door to the side of the room opened and a guard walked in. "Randy," she said, her voice sounding unnaturally loud. "I wondered where you were."

"Did you need something, Miss Timbers?"

"Yes...yes, I did," she said, laughing breathlessly. "I have to leave earlier than planned." She nodded toward the bags in her hands. "But I found...Mrs. Baxter—" her voice was positively cheerful as she hit on a name "—on the employees' staircase. She refused to go back to her room, Randy, and I simply don't have the time to persuade her."

"Don't you worry about it," he assured her. "I'll take care of everything."

She felt her knees grow weak. He was going to take care of it. He was going to leave the lounge.

But he didn't leave. Instead, he walked to a table and picked up the telephone. Amanda could have screamed. He stood with his back to the wall, his eyes traveling over the lounge as he punched in the correct numbers. His gaze drifted over the Boule cabinet, past it, then returned.

Amanda froze as he stared directly at the spot where Danny was hidden. Randy shook his head, covered the phone and said, "That picture always hangs crooked. Drives me crazy."

Then he turned around, facing the wall as he spoke into the telephone.

Rushing to open the front door, she motioned frantically for Danny. He had to pass right by the guard to reach the door, but he did it silently, his movements resembling those of a stalking lion.

Outside, she ran down the steps and to the waiting car. Unlocking the trunk, she shoved the carryall inside, then turned to Danny. "I...I never realized it was so small," she whispered, her voice scared. "I don't know—"

But Danny didn't wait to debate the size of the trunk. He climbed in, folding himself up agilely.

Closing the trunk lid was the hardest thing Amanda had ever done, but she couldn't give herself time to dwell on it. Running around to the front of the car, she threw her remaining bag into the back seat and slid in.

She had expected the tension to ease once they had actually left the house. But she was wrong. She constantly checked the rearview mirror, wondering when they would discover Danny's absence, wondering when she would see the lights of a car behind her.

Suddenly her headlights caught a rabbit as it ran directly in front of her. She slammed urgently on the brakes. Leaning her head forward, her breath came in sobs.

"I can't do it," she whispered in desperation. "I just can't do it."

Then she remembered Danny. He had more to lose than she had. He had the rest of his life to lose. Danny didn't deserve a coward.

Confront the dragon, she told herself once again. Easing the gearshift into drive, she began again. Almost at once, the gate was before her. She slowed, then came to a stop before it. She had never seen the man who stepped out of the brick-and-glass cage beside the gate. He wasn't the same guard who had admitted her that first day.

"Hello," she said as he reached the car. "I'm Amanda Timbers. Mrs. Oates said she would call to let you know I was leaving tonight."

The glare of a flashlight hit her face, and involuntarily she flinched.

"Can I see your driver's license, miss?"

After fumbling in her purse, Amanda handed him the license and had to endure the glare of the flashlight once more.

"Okay, Miss Timbers. You need to back the car up a few feet. The gates will swing this way." He turned to walk away... then stopped when a soft thud came from the trunk of the car.

Turning back, he glanced over the full length of the convertible. "Did you hear something?" he asked.

Her first instinct was to lie, but she squelched it. Nodding her head, she said, "I'm afraid I just threw everything in the trunk—I'm in a hurry—then about two miles back I almost hit a rabbit and slammed pretty hard on the brakes." Was she telling him too much? Did it sound natural? She shrugged. "I guess my things are shifting."

"Would you like me to check to see if anything is broken?" he asked.

"No...no, thank you. As I said, I'm in a hurry. My aunt is critically ill." She smiled. "There's nothing back there that could come to harm." *Only my life,* she added silently.

He nodded and seconds later the gates swung open. As she turned onto the macadam road, she heard the heavy gates clang shut behind her. Her hands were locked in a death grip on the steering wheel. She drove silently, desperately, always watching the odometer. After exactly five miles, she pulled over to the side of the road and parked.

Running to the trunk, she fumbled to open it, barely aware of the tears on her face. Danny stepped out and pulled her into his arms.

"It's all right, Mandy," he crooned softly. "Don't cry. I'll take care of you now."

Leaning away from him, she drew in a deep breath. They were free.

Chapter Nine

Hours and hours of I-15 passed by. Then, rising before them like the Emerald City, was Las Vegas. Its neon lights dazzled the eye and confused the mind. To Amanda, it was a little like being abruptly thrown from darkness into a psychedelic dream.

She had long gone past the point of exhaustion to a blessed numbness. With some rational part of her mind, she knew she needed to stop and rest, but she also knew she wouldn't feel easy until she and Danny were married. The legal tie between them was her safety net.

Pulling into a crowded parking lot, she switched off the motor and turned to the man beside her. "Well, Danny," she said, smiling lightly. "This is Las Vegas. What do you think of it?"

He looked around at the signs that flashed champagne glasses and dancing women and eight-foot bowling pins. Then he turned to watch a group of laughing, weaving people walking along the sidewalk.

"It feels loud," he said finally. "I like it. It's . . . it's alive."

She laughed. "It's that all right." She rested her chin on the steering wheel. "Danny, I didn't tell you part of my plan. I was waiting until now because . . . well, I guess because I'm a coward." Turning her head sideways, she met his questioning gaze. "You know that legally I had no right to help you leave Greenleigh."

After a moment, he said, "Dr. Sutherland is the boss and he wouldn't have let me leave."

"That's right. Only someone related to you could tell Dr. Sutherland to let you go." She swallowed heavily, finding the explanation even more difficult than she had anticipated. "You and I, we're not family— but there is a way that we could be."

He stared at her silently for a long time. She watched his changing expression and followed his thoughts almost as though he spoke aloud. He rejected several possibilities with a slight shake of his head, then, his voice unsure, he said, "Is a wife family?"

Nodding her head shortly, she said in relief, "Yes . . . yes, a wife is family." She reached out to touch his hand. "You know, you don't have to do anything you don't want to do. That's the first rule of our new life. You get a choice from now on. But if we were married, no one could put you back in Greenleigh unless I said they could."

"And you wouldn't do that."

There was no uncertainty in his voice now. The totality of his trust made her feel inadequate.

"I want to marry you, Mandy. Then we can always be together."

Always, she thought, biting her lip to keep it from trembling. For Danny, always would be too short a time.

"Okay," she said, inhaling deeply. "Then let's do it."

In the land of takeout weddings, it didn't take long to find what she was looking for. Standing on the sidewalk, Amanda winced when she stared at the bright, white-neon letters across the street. They shouted WEDDING CHAPEL to already satiated senses.

Wedding in Neon, she thought. It sounded like an off-Broadway play.

"It's beautiful," Danny said in awe as he gazed up at the huge letters and the trailing blue-neon ribbons. "It's like the whole town is glad to see us."

Amanda stared at him mutely. How did he always manage to find the good? She saw gaudy worldliness; he saw warm welcome. In that moment, she made a silent vow to try with everything that was in her to look at the world through Danny's eyes.

Suddenly, the chapel didn't look so harsh. Even the white-satin-attired minister and the plastic flowers adorning the small chapel couldn't put her off.

Two witnesses were included in the wedding fee. The disinterested but comfortable-looking women talked in low whispers about a pottery class they were both taking. The down-to-earth reality of them added sharp contrast to the unbelievable night.

No one seemed to think it strange that Amanda's blue-linen slacks were rumpled or that her face was lined with weariness. Or that Danny glanced around the room wide-eyed as he clenched his fist around the opal ring Amanda had removed from her right hand earlier.

For a while, the words of the ceremony flowed uncomprehended through the numbness of her mind, then gradually they began to take shape.

".. . to have and to hold from this day forward; to love and to cherish, in sickness and in health—"

She raised her eyes to Danny's as the last words fell into the silence.

"—till death us do part."

"Till death us do part," she whispered unsteadily. Sweet Jesus, she prayed in desperation. It wasn't fair. Death would come so soon. There would be no time for her and Danny. If the soul lingered after death, please, God, let hers linger near Danny's.

She felt a touch on her arm and glanced around. The minister and the witnesses were staring at her expectantly. The woman on her left side whispered, "You're supposed to say 'I do' now, honey."

Amanda swallowed the lump in her throat. "I do."

The words were barely a whisper, but they were enough. Now it was Danny's turn. He listened with solemn care as the same words were intoned, keeping his eyes trained on the minister's face. Then, slowly, he turned to Amanda, his gaze loving as it drifted over her face. Reaching out, he cupped her cheek with a gentle hand.

"I do, Mandy." The words were soft and husky. "I do take you."

Before the minister had finished pronouncing them man and wife, Danny lowered his head and brushed his lips across hers. Amanda placed her hand over his, closing her eyes as she pressed it tightly to her face.

She felt a terrible weight dissolve. They were married, she kept telling herself over and over as they walked out of the chapel to the offhand good wishes of the witnesses and minister. They were married. The license was in her purse. No one could force Danny to go anywhere or do anything without her consent.

"We did it, Danny," she said as they drove away. Her voice was filled with excitement and the laughter of relief. "We really did it."

Laughing with her, he laid his large hand on her thigh, not in a sensual move but in a gesture of affection and camaraderie; they were in it together, for good and for bad.

Amanda's vision was blurring when she pulled the car into the parking lot of a motel on the interstate. The sign that flashed messages to passing cars and the neon palm tree looked familiar now and even homey.

Danny stood at her side as she paid for one night's lodging, then together, they carried their bags to the small room. Amanda was too tired even to speak as they laid the bags on the twin beds. She pulled out her nightgown and walked into the white-tiled bathroom.

When she returned, Danny was already in bed, his strong, bare back turned toward her. After switching off the light, she climbed wearily into the bed, her sore body fighting the characteristic stiffness of the mattress and pillow.

She had expected to fall asleep immediately, but her mind was too full. When Danny shifted his position, it was a restless sound.

"I've been thinking," he said quietly, as though continuing a conversation.

"Me too," she whispered. "Too much has happened. I imagine it's been even more confusing for you."

"Everything is new. It's exciting...." His voice trailed off in the darkness.

"But?"

He shifted again. "I don't know very much. I didn't even know there was so much to know." He paused. "You paid for the room. I don't know about money."

She heard the quiet frustration in his voice. "You'll learn," she said, her voice determined. "No one has been teaching you. That's my job now. We'll start tomorrow with money. Soon I'll teach you how to drive the car and use a pay telephone and anything else you want to know."

"I want to know everything," he said flatly.

Her laugh was soft with affection. "I'm afraid even I don't know everything. But I'll teach you what I know, then we'll find someone who can teach you the rest."

He exhaled, and the sound was loud in the dark room. "You make it sound like I can really do it."

"Of course you can do it," she said firmly, almost angrily. "We're alike, remember? Neither of us is perfect, but we have something better than perfection. We've got hard heads; we don't give up. Right?"

"Right," he said, laughing huskily.

Silence mingled with the hum of the air conditioner and after a while Amanda decided he had fallen asleep. She forced her body to relax because she knew she needed her rest. They had a long hard drive ahead of them tomorrow.

"Mandy?" His voice was a mere whisper, soft and wistful in the darkness.

"Yes?"

"It scares me to think about not knowing you. When I look at you ... when I look at you my heart smiles. You make me more," he finished simply.

She closed her eyes tightly and tried to keep her voice steady. "We make each other more, Danny. Don't ever forget that. You give me as much as I give you. This is not just a beginning for you. It's also the beginning of the rest of my life."

"What will it be like?"

"It will be whatever we want to make it. You'll like the cabin. It's not very big, but there are no fences around it. There's not a thing there to keep life out."

The sound of her own voice acted as a sedative, and as she slowly talked of their new life, they both fell asleep.

Amanda stared down at the syringe for a long time. "Danny," she said, her voice shaky. "Danny, I'm scared."

"Just stick me," he said. His voice was matter-of-fact as he sat on the bed and watched her. "You did it before and it didn't hurt...honest." He grinned. "Pretend I'm a dragon, then you won't mind sticking me."

Straightening her back, she inserted the needle into the rubber top of the vial, then turned it upside down to draw the drug inside. She had put this off until last. Their bags were packed and in the car. They were ready to go.

Turning around, she walked to the bed. She had already prepared his right upper arm for the intramuscular shot. There was nothing left to do but give it. Holding her breath she plunged the needle into the muscle. Danny didn't even jerk. He simply waited patiently until she was through.

"You did fine," he said, rolling down his sleeve.

"I think I need some breakfast...or a stiff drink," she said wryly.

His laughter reassured her, and suddenly she really did feel hungry. They had breakfast at the small coffee shop attached to the motel. While they were waiting for their orders, Amanda began teaching Danny. He recognized numbers and was quick to understand what she told him, which pleased them both. It was a good start.

Several hours later, when they stopped for gas, Amanda turned half of their cash over to Danny. After separating a ten-dollar bill from his pile, Danny stepped from the car and told the teenage attendant to put ten dollars' worth in the car.

Giving him an encouraging smile, she left him by himself and went to get cold drinks from a machine beside the station. She dawdled purposely, understanding how important this simple transaction was to him. Then, as she walked back toward the pumps, the irate voice of the attendant reached her.

"What are you—some kind of dummy? I don't know where the ten went, but I know you're gonna pay for this gas. Judas priest, man, just give me two fives or ten ones. It don't have to be a ten-dollar bill."

Amanda ran the rest of the way. When she reached the two men she stooped to pick up the ten-dollar bill from beneath the car and shoved it into the hand of the teenager.

"What do you think you're doing?" she said, her voice low and stiff with fury. "I want your name and your manager's telephone number, and I want them *now*. Your behavior is inexcusable. You have no right to be serving the public. If I have to—" She broke off when the felt Danny's hand on her arm.

"Mandy," he said softly. "Let's go. I want to get to the cabin."

She exhaled slowly, then nodded and turned away. She drove the car automatically, anger still holding her in its grip long after they had left the gas station behind.

"You're still mad," Danny said sadly, breaking the tense silence. "I didn't do very well."

She glanced at him quickly. "Don't say that. You did just fine. It was that idiot kid who made me mad. What kind of parents does he have? Didn't anyone

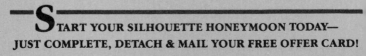

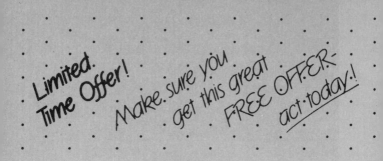

Limited
Time Offer!

Make sure you get this great FREE OFFER— act today!

ever teach him manners? He's got the sensitivity of a warthog in heat.''

Danny was silent for a moment, then he said quietly, "Will he be living with us?''

She jerked her gaze toward him in confusion. "Of course not.''

He smiled. "Then it doesn't matter, does it?''

She almost sagged as she felt the tension leave her body. Laughing softly, she said, "You're right. He's not important. We're together, and that's what counts.''

As if by magic, the incident was behind them. They were on their way to a new life. She couldn't let anything spoil it now.

Flat Nevada highway stretched before them, and it was growing dark when they began to enter the mountainous area that would lead them to their new home.

Now that it was over, now that they were nearing the isolated mountain cabin, Amanda began to have doubts for the first time since they had left Greenleigh.

She couldn't tell whether the doubts came now because she finally had time to think or because she was so bone-achingly tired. Had she done the right thing? What right did she have to tamper with his life, his health? Who in hell did she think she was?

Before the thoughts could drive her crazy, the cabin appeared out of the darkness, looking small and deserted in the headlights. But it would be just as she remembered it, sturdy and safe nestled among towering trees.

Switching off the engine, she turned to the man beside her. "We're here," she said softly, unnecessarily.

He stared at the cabin in silence, then stepped from the car. A frown worried her lips. She felt more than a physical withdrawal from him. Did he regret coming with her? Or was he simply as tired as she was?

Together they took the bags and boxes of provisions they'd bought into the cabin. "Just a second and I'll find the lanterns. It's chilly here. I didn't expect that. If there's wood we'll have a fire."

She was talking too much. She knew it, but she couldn't stop. Running her fingers through her hair, she tried to think. One thing at a time, she told herself. Just get through one thing at a time.

Under the sink, she found three lanterns and the water cutoff. She could wait until the next day to light the water heater, she decided. Her hands trembled as she lit the kerosene lanterns. It was a miracle she had remembered to buy more fuel. She placed the lanterns around the room, then turned to look around the cabin.

It was merely one large room, but it held everything they needed. Arranged around the room were a wide, old-fashioned bed, a couch against the front wall, a brown fur rug before the small, stone fireplace, and four chairs pulled up to a small, wooden dining table.

On the right side of the front door was the kitchenette. There were several hand tools on the counter where her father had left them the last time he'd been here. Strangely, they eased her tension. They made her feel at home, as though any minute her father would walk through the door.

"It'll do, Danny," she murmured. "It'll do."

She moved to a chest and took out sheets, pillows and blankets. "The lid fits tight," she said over her shoulder. "They don't even smell musty. Not that I would have noticed." She pushed her hair back with one hand. "I don't know about you, but I'm dead tired."

Suddenly she dropped the covers to the bed and her shoulders drooped wearily. "Oh, Danny," she whispered as much to herself as to him. "I'm so scared. It's got to be all right."

But still he didn't speak, and when she had smoothed the blanket twice, she turned around to face him. "Danny, what's wrong?" she asked quietly. "Don't you like the cabin? Would you rather go somewhere else?"

He simply stood and stared at her. Raising her chin, she met his eyes. Then she drew in a sharp breath. His eyes were green, this time a frightening-looking green. The only time she had seen him look like this was when Ginny had forgotten to give him—

Oh God! she thought, going weak with fear. Danny's medication! She had forgotten his evening medication.

"Oh, no," she whispered. "I'm so sorry. Danny, I forgot your injection." Tears of weariness and self-blame sprang to her eyes. "It's the most important thing and I forgot."

Moving quickly to the table, she opened the carry-all and pulled out two boxes—the syringes and the drug. Her hands shook as she opened the boxes.

"I'll take care of it right now, then you'll be all right— Damn it, calm down," she whispered harshly to herself. "I hope you can forgive me, Danny, because it's going to be very hard to forgive myself."

Not a single word did he speak as she turned the vial upside down and carefully drew in the right amount. "Now," she said, turning around. "We'll fix—"

Danny stood directly behind her, one hand raised above his head, the metal head of the hammer he held glinting dully in the lantern light.

She felt her heart leap and instinctively backed against the table. Before she could react, he knocked the vial and the needle from her hands in a vicious backhand swipe. Then, staring straight at her, he reached out.

"Danny—" she began, then stopped. This is the end, she told herself in resignation. Strangely, fear never entered her mind. Not even when she remembered Ginny's words that first day. "He was out to do murder."

Oh, Danny, she thought, *what have I done to you?*

When he grasped her by the throat, Amanda merely stood still, waiting. Then with an almost careless motion, he pushed her aside and brought the hammer down violently onto the carryall...and the vials of medication it contained.

"Danny!" She grabbed his arm. "No, you can't!"

He shook her off with no effort at all and continued to bring the hammer down, again and again as the sound of breaking glass filled the room.

"No, no, no," she said, sobbing as she struggled with him again. This time, when he shook her off she landed on her knees. Pulling herself to her feet, she saw the carryall, saturated with the precious drug. It was too late.

She lowered her face to her hands. It had all been for nothing, and she had no one to blame but herself.

Her head jerked up when she heard a loud crash. He had moved away from the table. Standing before a heavy wooden-framed mirror, he slammed the hammer into the glass. He wasn't merely out of control; he was enraged, as though he wanted to destroy himself. Suddenly, slinging the hammer across the room, he began to use his fist on what was left of the mirror.

She watched in horror as blood flew onto the wall and the floor. Without thinking, she was on her feet. She rushed at him, throwing her body against his, shoving with all her might.

If he hadn't already been off balance, she probably wouldn't have affected him at all. But she caught him as he turned, and her weight, with running force behind it, carried him to the bed and they fell across it together.

He twisted, trying to get up, trying to get away from her clinging arms. But she had already done enough damage. She couldn't let anything else happen to him.

His struggles grew weaker. She could feel his strength ebbing and cradled his head against her breast, crooning like a mother over a sick child. She felt his body give in to the total relaxation of sleep, and still she didn't let him go. The hands that stroked his face and his back continued to move, slower and slower.

She wasn't fully conscious when she rose from the bed. Seconds later, she began cleaning and bandaging his hands. She was even too tired to cry when she saw the deep, ragged cuts on his knuckles and palms. Once she had them tightly wrapped, she took his hands in hers and held them against her face, rocking back and forth.

Just then he stirred and groaned in his sleep, and she slid down beside him, wrapping her arms around his waist. "It's all right, Danny," she whispered, her voice so hoarse it was barely audible. "I'm here. I'm here."

She would clean up the cabin in a minute, she told herself. She would try to think, try to decide what to do, in a minute. She would . . .

She didn't manage to complete the thought before sleep claimed her.

Amanda was dreaming. Strangely, she was aware that it was a dream, but she didn't care. It was the most beautiful dream she had ever had. She and Danny were walking in the woods. The sun was shining, streaming down through the trees, turning everything golden.

She had never felt so happy, so carefree. Danny was laughing and talking, communicating without effort, free at last of the dreadful hesitation.

Then, with love shining from his green eyes, he picked her up and whirled her around. In slow motion they fell together to the soft grass. Their eyes met for an endless moment, then Danny was kissing her, touching her, loving her.

She moved into each caress, feeling his warmth surround her. In the way of dreams, their clothes melted away, and they were lying naked together in the grass, the warm sun stroking their limbs.

The fire inside her blazed and grew fierce. She placed her slender hands over the large ones at her breasts and pressed them closer, moving her lower body against the strength of his.

Moaning, she felt the heat of him press against her. She needed more, infinitely more. She needed it all.

Later, she was never sure when the dream merged with reality. She knew her eyes were open. She knew Danny's strong, hard body was pressed against hers, the naked flesh searing her. She may have even begun to protest. But at that moment, his lips covered hers, and it was so achingly beautiful, she lost all thought. She could only feel. His touch banished any objection she might have made in a saner moment. There was no regret, no shame now. Too much power and beauty were contained in their loving to allow the existence of such weak emotions.

When he entered her at last, Amanda cried out with the agonizing sweetness of it. They merged and became one entity in search of a single goal.

As the tension built, she reached desperately for something just beyond her grasp, the suddenly, explosively, she found it, and it took her away from reality, giving her a taste of immortality.

She was only half-conscious when she felt Danny reach down and pull the covers over them both. She smiled. He was taking care of her. Then she fell asleep again.

The day was gray with early-morning mist when she woke again. She began to stretch, then she remembered. No matter how she tried, she couldn't stop a momentary feeling of guilt. But, stubbornly, she rejected it. It was right. She and Danny belonged together. She didn't care what the world would think of them because so often the world was wrong. Only she and Danny were qualified to judge what they had together.

It was only then, when she felt strength and purpose enter her, that she remembered the medication. Catching her breath, she turned her head and found herself gazing into the cold, angry eyes of a stranger.

Chapter Ten

Daniel Phillips stared into the eyes of the woman lying beside him. He held his gaze steady, fighting his chaotic thoughts.

Think calmly, he told himself, shifting his gaze to the room around him. There was an explanation for everything.

He could feel the woman watching him closely and returned his gaze to her. Suddenly he frowned. Why did she look frightened?

"Who are you?" he asked, his voice raspy.

Her blue eyes clouded with the question. Why did it disturb her so much? Moving abruptly, he threw back the cover and picked up the clothes from the floor beside the bed, his eyes trained on the woman as he pulled them on.

The clothes were his; logic told him that. But he didn't recognize them any more than he recognized the woman.

Suddenly his movements stopped. One sleeve of the white shirt was smeared with blood. For the first time, he noticed the bandages on his hands.

Daniel didn't move. It was very important that he not let her know how panicky he felt. If he pretended to be sane, he told himself, sanity would come. There was an explanation for everything, he told himself again. All he had to do was find it.

Lord, he thought, running a hand through his hair, he must have gone on the bender of all benders last night. All the times he had dunked Kyle's head under cold water to sober him came back to Daniel. Was this how his brother had felt the morning after?

A movement caught his peripheral vision. Bringing his gaze back to the woman on the bed, he saw her inhale deeply, then she threw back the blanket she had held clutched to her breasts and stepped from the bed.

Daniel drew in a sharp breath. Even drunk, he hadn't lost his taste. She was perfect. Her breasts were round and firm, the rest of her body small and shapely. The creamy texture of her skin shone in the morning light.

"Could you not watch me so closely?" she asked quietly, interrupting his examination.

With an effort, he glanced away. Her voice was as soft as her skin looked. But he was puzzled by her attitude. Had she been drunk the night before also? Was their togetherness as much a surprise to her as it was to him?

Lord, he thought suddenly, he hoped he hadn't promised her anything. That was the kind of stunt his brother pulled, much to the regret of Daniel's bank.

When the rustle of clothing stopped, Daniel turned back to the woman. He stared at her for a moment in silence, then he shrugged his stiff shoulder muscles.

"I'm afraid you're going to have to fill me in on a few things," he said quietly, struggling to sound sure of himself. "I seem to have lost last night...no reflections on your charm, I'm sure."

Briefly, she closed her eyes, as though something he said had hurt her. He frowned. "Who are you?" he asked again. "How did we get here?" He glanced around the room. "Just exactly where are we?"

She cleared her throat nervously. "I'm Man— Amanda Timbers. We're in Nevada. We drove here last night after we left Greenleigh."

He frowned as a sharp pain pierced his temple. Rubbing his brow, he searched his memory, trying to recall this woman. What was Greenleigh? And what was he doing in Nevada? But it was no use. The last thing he could remember was seeing his father off on a business trip. He and Kyle had stood together, watching the private jet take off from the small landing strip....

"For crissake, Dan, will you get a move on."

Daniel didn't even glance at his brother. He stared after the plane until it disappeared in the cloudy distance.

"Gina's coming to pick me up in an hour," Kyle said, "and I'm here giving Dad the grand goodbye. I knew I should have brought the Jag."

Daniel turned reluctantly away from the stretch of tarmac. "Sam said they would probably run into turbulence over Colorado," he said, his voice distracted.

"The old man knows what he's doing," Kyle said as they walked toward the waiting limousine. "And Sam has been his pilot for a lot of years. He wouldn't take off if there was a real problem. Do you think you can keep the plane out of trouble? Lighten up for heaven's sake." As they stepped into the back of the car, Kyle said to the driver, "Don't spare the horses, Carlo. I've got a date with an angel."

"They're all angels to you," Daniel said, chuckling.

"Gina's different." Kyle glanced at his watch. "I would have been home already if I had brought my own car."

"That Jaguar will kill you one of these days, then the only angel you'll have to worry about is the one with the book of records."

Kyle made a rude gesture. "Will you stop trying to take care of the whole world, big brother? You worry about Dad; you worry about me. Work and worry— that's what will kill you . . . or make you lose your hair."

Daniel smiled. "No big loss. I don't have cute curls that drive women wild."

"It's not only my curls that drive women wild. They know that if they stick with Kyle Phillips, the sky's the limit. Why don't you stop being such a sourpuss and let me fix you up with Gina's roommate? She's got legs that would stop a truck.''

Daniel shook his head, laughing at his brother's exaggerated expression of lust. "I believe I'll pass on the legs...if you'll remember, I'm a breast man. Besides, I think there's some kind of rule that says there can only be one heartthrob per family. If I became one too, it would throw nature off balance.''

Daniel thought of the conversation later as he stood in the doorway of his study and waved good-night to Kyle and Gina. His brother was twenty-one, but at times Daniel wondered if Kyle's brain had caught up with his body. He liked to see Kyle have a good time, but he wondered what would happen when it was time for him to settle down. Would he be able to hold his own in the business world?

Walking back into the study, he sat behind a wide walnut desk. With a frown, he accepted part of the responsibility for Kyle's behavior. Early in his life, he had gotten into the habit of taking care of his brother. Someday Kyle would have to learn to take care of himself.

Shaking his head, he picked up a paper from the desk. His best course would be to take Kyle's advice and stop worrying. His brother was adored by every woman he met and liked by every man. His charm was irresistible. Daniel grinned. Kyle would make a damn good used-car salesman.

Leaning back in the tall leather chair, he decided he and his brother had each been given certain gifts at the moment of conception. Kyle's was the ability to get along well with others. Daniel's gift was the ability to look at an idea and assess its value. Work was his specialty. He would have to take care to use that gift, now and in the future.

The future...

The pain in his temple spread to become a throbbing ache. He walked stiffly a few paces forward then caught his reflection in a piece of the shattered mirror that hung on the wall. Something was very wrong, he thought, his pulse beating erratically. He glanced up to find the woman watching him closely.

"How old am I?" he asked abruptly as a vague suspicion took shape.

"Thirty-nine."

He closed his eyes tightly. *Thirty-nine!* He didn't doubt her because somehow he had known. He was remembering his life when he was twenty-eight. Eleven years were missing. Damn it, eleven years gone as though they had never existed.

"Somehow I get the idea I didn't pick you up in a bar," he said dryly, then glanced away from the pain in her eyes. "Tell me everything you know," he said, the words coming out harsh. "Tell me how we met. What I was doing. Don't leave anything out."

He had to get it straightened out. He had to know. Whether he liked it or not, this woman was the only immediate link to his past.

She sat on the bed, staring at the slender hands that were folded in her lap. "I've known you for a couple of months," she said quietly. "I met you when I took a job as bookkeeper at Greenleigh Acres."

"Greenleigh Acres? You said that before. What exactly is it?"

"It's—" She broke off, looking uncomfortable. "It's a kind of resort. You had been...ill for about six months before I met you."

"Be specific," he said tightly. "What kind of illness?"

She drew in a long breath and closed her eyes. "You have a degenerative brain disease," she said in a rush. "When I met you, you had the mental capacity of a six-year-old child."

Moving quickly, she knelt beside him, her blue eyes showing panic. "I took you out," she said urgently. "It was wrong because I forgot to give you your medication and... Oh God, they said you couldn't live without it. I've got to take you back. Last night you smashed all the drug I had. We've got to go back before it's too late. I can't—"

"That's enough," he said, grabbing her shoulders. "Calm down."

"But—"

"Shut up," he said, his voice harsh. "Let me think a minute."

He glanced at the satchel on the table, at the broken glass spilling from it. Surveying the room, he saw again the broken mirror. Had he done that? He must have gone crazy.

He forced himself to think logically. He could beat this, he told himself. All he had to do was stay calm.

Meeting her gaze, he said, "If this brain disorder is degenerative, why is my mind all right today? The only thing wrong with me is my memory. That will come back as soon as my head is clearer." It had to, he added silently.

She stood, walked two steps away, then swung back to face him. "I don't know what's happening. That's what scares me so much. It could be some kind of remission. Ted said no one knew how the brain worked." Her lower lip trembled slightly, making her look vulnerable. "But you could be in a period of lucidity before—" She broke off, closing her eyes tightly.

"Before death," he finished with a sardonic smile.

"Damn you!" she said, rounding on him. "Don't you dare smile. My God, you're a cold-blooded bastard. Can't you see I'm terrified? If anything happens, it's my fault. I'm the one who convinced you to leave."

His eyes narrowed speculatively. "Why would you do something like that?"

She rubbed her neck, avoiding his eyes. "I found out that people with your disease—Sutherland's Complex—only live for approximately two years after the first symptoms appear." She shrugged. "I decided... I decided if you had to die, you should do it in freedom."

"You took a lot on yourself," he murmured, wondering about her motives. There was something she wasn't telling him. "Who's Ted?"

She looked exhausted as she brushed her hair back with one hand. "Dr. Ted Sutherland. He owns Greenleigh. He discovered your disorder and developed a drug that would halt its progress... temporarily."

He added the information to his scanty supply. For a few moments he was silent. Then he glanced up. "You sound sincere. In fact, you almost convince me—"

"Thank you so much," she muttered, her eyes blazing.

"—but not quite," he finished as though she hadn't spoken. "Too much doesn't fit. What kind of doctor would turn a patient over to a bookkeeper? And what about my father and Kyle? You're not trying to tell me you took me with their blessing?"

"Kyle?"

His lips tightened. He had almost begun to believe she was merely confused, but she was pretending she didn't know about Kyle.

"My brother," he said coldly. "Who are you? You couldn't be from this Greenleigh place, or you would know Kyle."

She shook her head, frowning. "I didn't know. They told me you hadn't had a visitor in the six months before I arrived. I... I just assumed you had no family."

He studied her silently. "Okay, let's say you're telling the truth. That still doesn't explain why they turned me over to you."

"They didn't," she whispered. There was only a minute pause, then she glanced up, meeting his eyes with her chin raised. "I took you out in the trunk of my car."

He leaned back in the chair, his eyes narrowing. "It seems we had quite an adventure. I'm sorry I can't remember it." The look she gave him was almost hateful. "So out of the goodness of your heart, you decided to make an idiot's last days happy. Is that the way it was?"

"Don't say that!" she said furiously. "Danny wasn't—you weren't an idiot." She ran a trembling hand across her face. "I can't explain. It hit me hard when I found out he...when I found out you were going to die. I simply couldn't stand the way you were stashed away in that luxurious prison. John called it a velvet zoo. They took care of you and gave you everything you needed, but no one talked to you or listened to you. They watched every move you made. They treated you as though, because your brain was damaged, you had no emotions, no human dignity."

He was silent for a moment, considering her explanation. "Who is John?"

She smiled. "He's a wonderful old man. Danny...you called him John J. Pike. Never John or even Mr. Pike. It was always John J. Pike."

"You seem to have split me into two people," he said wryly. "You called me Danny then."

She nodded and turned away, but not before he saw the sheen of tears in her eyes. "You're not two people," she whispered, her voice husky. "Danny's gone." Her hands clenched into fists. "And I'm so scared for him."

She swung around. "We've got to do something. The best medical men in the country said you had extensive brain damage. We can't doubt that. You seem to be an intelligent, logical man. If this is some sort of remission, then the doctors need to know about it. It may help others. But if it's not...if your condition is getting worse, then you need immediate medical attention."

He took in what she was saying, letting it sink in, trying to make sense of it. But it was impossible. Nothing had made sense since he had awoken to find her lying naked beside him. The remembered warmth made him look at her more closely.

"In a morning full of strange happenings, I find you strangest of all," he murmured, not knowing whether he was talking to himself or her. "What kind of person would do the kind of things you've told me you've done?"

"An ordinary person," she said, her very beauty denying the simple statement.

"That's not enough. Do you have some kind of martyr complex? I've seen that before. It's not healthy for anyone concerned. What were your plans for me— or rather for Danny? What about the future?

She inhaled slowly. "As I've told you over and over, I thought he was going to die. There was no future for Danny. A year or two at the most."

"Two years can be a long time," he said quietly, remembering times and places in the past. "Surely you weren't planning on living here in rural splendor for all that time. Why would you cut yourself off from everyone for a—"

"Don't you dare call him an idiot again!" she snapped.

Daniel shook his head ruefully. "I find this a very strange conversation. It's a little hard for me to keep up with the characters."

She stared at him, anger and maybe even curiosity in her gaze. "How can you talk about it like that? This is not a play. This is all about you . . . about whether you live or die. I just don't understand you."

"Snap," he said dryly. "We seem to have reached some kind of impasse. I don't understand you and you don't understand me. But like you said, it's my life we're talking about. I think that entitles me to call the shots."

"Without even knowing the facts?" she asked in disbelief. "How can you do anything until you know what's going on? That's like driving a car blindfolded." She threw out an emphatic arm. "Disregard everything else I've told you if you like. But at least believe that you need medical attention and you need it *now*."

For a moment he couldn't look away from her adamant face. Then he stood and began to pace back and forth, ignoring the way she watched him.

What if she was right? he thought, frowning. Shouldn't he at least be examined by a doctor so that he could know what he was dealing with?

Turning abruptly, he knocked her purse off the counter and stooped to pick up the scattered items.

"Don't worry about that," she said hastily, rushing to kneel beside him. "I'll take care of it." She reached for the folded piece of paper he held in his hand.

Daniel met her gaze and held it for a long moment. Then shifting his eyes to the paper, he unfolded it. The silence between them drew out and became electric with tension as he slowly read the words printed there.

When he raised his eyes to the woman beside him, they both stood, staring at each other warily.

"It seems there was something you forgot to tell me," he said softly, glancing again at what appeared to be his own marriage license.

Chapter Eleven

He looked so cold, Amanda thought, feeling a wave of dizziness pass through her. So very cold and so very angry. Wiping her damp palms on the sides of her slacks, she glanced around the room. Anywhere but at him. How could she possibly explain? It had been difficult explaining to Danny, who loved her. This man would never understand.

Bracing herself, she met his eyes. "I know it looks strange—"

"To say the least," he said dryly.

She drew in a deep breath. "Yes, well. At the time it seemed the right thing to do. At least, it was the only thing I could think of. You're not a man who could just disappear without notice. I thought if we were married I would have some say in the way you were treated." She raised her small chin defiantly. "I know it was wrong, but I had already done enough to get me thrown in jail. I didn't see why I should balk at marriage."

Reluctantly, Daniel felt a touch of admiration. She had guts. But a lot of dishonest, unscrupulous people had guts, he reminded himself, and all the facts were against her. She had married a man—a very wealthy, very powerful man—who, if she was to be believed, was incapable of making a rational decision at the time.

Amanda saw the suspicion grow in his dark-green eyes and turned away from him. Couldn't he see that none of this was important? Guilt and fear were twisting her insides, making her physically ill. What if she had done Danny—no, not Danny, she thought as a sharp pain shot through her. What if she had done this man irreparable harm?

She swung around to face him. "None of that matters now. I don't know what's happening to you, but we've got to get you back to Dr. Sutherland so he can check you." She clenched her fists. "Don't you see? You could be dying?"

He stared at her in silence. After a moment he walked to the table and picked up the car keys. "Neither of us is going anywhere. Not until I've figured out what's going on." He raised a hand to his head, rubbing his temple. He couldn't explain it, even to himself. but he knew he couldn't go back. Not yet.

"I've got to think," he said harshly. "I've got to work it all out."

She moved toward him. "What's wrong? Oh, God, you look white. Come lie down on the bed."

He shook off her hand. "Just leave me alone."

She bit her lip. "Put the keys in your pocket. I won't be able to get them without you waking up. You've got to get some rest."

Without responding, he moved to the couch and sat down, leaning his head back against the wall. He looked so weak, Amanda thought as she sat at the table, her gaze never leaving him.

After a while, although he fought it, he fell asleep. Immediately Amanda relaxed. Leaning forward, she rested her head on her forearm and studied him as he slept.

He almost looked like Danny, she thought, now that those cold, green eyes were hidden.

Suddenly she closed her eyes tightly. What was she thinking? Of course he looked like Danny. He *was* Danny. But her confusion was understandable. Even his features had changed. This man was attractive— cynical and somewhat cold, but attractive. But he was nothing like Danny. The lines in his face were deeper, but it was his expression rather than the lines that made him look harder and older.

The man on the couch moved restlessly in his sleep, as though he were uncomfortable, bringing her attention back to him instantly.

Moving quietly, she walked to the couch and picked up a cushion from the floor. She placed it beside him at the end of the couch, then turned him gently until he was stretched out full length.

Although he groaned softly, he didn't wake. They had been through a lot. He must have been dead tired, she thought, brushing her dark hair back wearily as she stood beside the couch and stared down at him.

And so was she. But tired or not, she would have to stop jumping every time he moved, every time he looked at her. If only she could forget what Ted and Ginny had told her. She was desperately afraid something would happen to him, but there was nothing she could do about it. He had made a decision, and she was forced to abide by it.

She stretched her aching back muscles, glancing around the cabin. It was a mess, but then so was she. And for a moment, she didn't care.

But habit of cleanliness was too strongly ingrained for her to resist. She decided if she moved quietly she wouldn't disturb him while she cleaned.

I've got to get out. Oh God, I'm suffocating.

Daniel was in an enormous room, surrounded by luxury, all grotesquely overdone. Chandeliers as big as pianos hung from the ceiling, and the furniture gleamed of gold. People in ornate costumes milled around the room, each of them looking straight through Daniel as though he weren't there.

He had no idea where he was, but he knew he hated the place and was terrified by it. He began moving quickly through the laughing, talking people, pushing them aside, looking for a way out. But each door he tried opened onto the same room again. He always ended where he had begun. There was no way out. Angry shouts erupted from his throat.

No one heard. Suddenly, he knew that they didn't hear because he didn't exist. The elaborate room swam around him crazily, a kaleidoscope of whirling colors and hideous laughing faces.

Then the whirling stopped. Across the room he saw Amanda. He walked toward her, his movements sluggish as though his legs were weighted. He had to see her. It was important that he see what was in her eyes, but the closer he got, the more she pulled back into the shadows. Gasping for breath, he reached out to her....

Daniel awoke with a jerk. Cold sweat covered his body. He didn't move; he simply lay there, listening to the sound of his harsh breathing. The dream was still with him, overlying reality like the stale, sour smell of a room the day after a party.

It was the naked singularity, he thought suddenly, his mind still sluggish. It was a nonplace where law was suspended.

A noise broke through the residue of fear, and he turned his head slightly. She walked out of the bathroom, a towel wrapped around her slender body.

Daniel felt desire shoot through him and almost laughed. At least that part of him was functioning all right. He wanted to get up and throw her on the floor. At this point, violence would be very satisfying.

But he had the feeling violence wouldn't last long once he touched her. She was too beautiful, too desirable. He had to be wary of her. Until he put together the pieces of the past, he had to be wary of everyone and everything. In a world turned upside down, he couldn't even trust his own instincts.

Amanda felt him watching her even before she turned her head toward him. Her heart jumped in her chest then started to pound. The look in his eyes made her mouth go dry. This was different from Danny. Danny had looked at her with wistful longing, with the tenderness of love. This was naked, unyielding desire.

Clutching the towel more tightly around her, she pulled clean clothes from her suitcase. Then, without glancing in his direction, she went back to the bathroom. With carefully controlled movements, she closed the door behind her, then sank back against it, trembling in violent reaction.

She had to get control of herself. Whether either of them liked it or not, this man was still her responsibility.

Pushing away from the door, she began to dress. Later, when she reentered the room, Daniel was walking restlessly around the cabin, examining every inch silently as though it would give him a vital clue. For all the notice he paid her, he could have been alone.

"You've never been here before," she told him quietly.

"It's your cabin?" he said, glancing at her.

She nodded. "My parents gave it to me when they moved to Europe. This is the first time I've used it since then."

He frowned, rubbing his temple. "Europe?"

"What's wrong?"

He moved to stand at the window. "Europe," he said again. "That's why Kyle didn't come to see me. He's in Europe."

"You're remembering?"

He shook his head as though annoyed with himself. "Just that bit. Kyle moved to Italy to take over our operation there and I took over here in the States. That was after—" He broke off abruptly.

Amanda stared at him. "Is something wrong?"

"I took over the U.S. operations after my father died," he said, his voice calm and unfeeling, as though he were discussing a business problem. Then she saw the muscle beside his mouth twitch.

"I'm sorry," she murmured. "It must be like having it happen all over again."

Like it was happening all over again, he thought, repressing a shudder. He felt the same shock he had felt then. His father had never made it home from that business trip. The turbulence his pilot had expected over Colorado had turned into an unusually violent thunderstorm. Lightning had struck the jet even as Sam was calling for landing instructions.

Daniel had maintained his strength only because he knew his brother needed him. Kyle had been hit so hard....

"No more, Kyle." Daniel pulled his brother's hand down as the younger man signaled for another drink. The small bar in which they sat was not the kind of place either of them regularly patronized. The crowded room had not one ounce of charm; it was a place for getting drunk.

"Bourbon won't bring him back. No matter how much of it you drink." Daniel's voice was hard in an attempt to disguise his own pain. The will had been read that morning—cold, dead words were all that was left of their father. The rapidity of events had left them both dazed.

Kyle looked up at his brother, his eyes bewildered and bruised. "What am I going to do now, Dan? Why did he give the Italian operation to me? I've only been there twice, for God's sake."

Daniel stared down at his hands. "He was planning on sending you there this year to get used to it. But he expected to be around to help you." He glanced up. "You don't have to take it, Kyle. We've got controlling interest; we can sell off the holdings in Italy. You can stay here and work with me."

"Don't you mean for you?" Kyle asked, an uncharacteristic cynicism entering his voice. "He gave Philton to you. I don't think I would like being your flunky."

"Kyle..."

His brother shook his head stubbornly. "No. I'll go to Rome, and I'll do the job he wanted me to do." He smiled suddenly. "How about a contest, big brother? You give me five years, and I'll make Phil-Ital worth twice what Philton is worth."

Daniel smiled slightly. "It'll take a little while to get used to seeing you as a business opponent, but I'm willing to make a small wager."

Kyle's laughter was a little too loud, a little too forced. "This calls for a celebration." Glancing around, he spotted the waitress busy at another table. "To show what a good sport I am, I'll get the drinks. Next time you can buy in honor of your defeat."

Daniel leaned back, watching Kyle walk unsteadily to the bar. It was at times like these that he felt the difference between him and his brother. Sometimes he felt that difference had put a distance between them. It was probably the same for all brothers. When they became adults, individuality took over, and brotherhood took a back seat. The ties would always be there, but only in the background of each of their lives.

Shifting in his chair, he glanced up as angry voices brought his attention to the bar.

"Hell, man, how did I know she was with you? She didn't seem to mind giving me a little kiss." Kyle smiled down at the girl on the bar stool beside him. "Did you, darling?"

A very large, very angry man reached out to grab Kyle's collar roughly. "You keep your hands and your smart mouth to yourself, pretty boy, or I'll arrange to have your fingers repossessed."

Daniel shoved back his chair and walked to the bar. Slowly, firmly, he loosened the man's grip on Kyle. "My brother sincerely apologizes," he said quietly. "He's had a few too many and mistook the lady's friendly smile for an invitation. It was an honest mistake."

Reaching out to shake the man's hand, Daniel slipped him a twenty-dollar bill. The hesitation left the man's face as he pushed the bill into his pocket. His back was turned when Daniel led his brother from the bar.

Kyle began laughing as soon as the door closed behind them. "Did you see his face? Lord, did you see *her* face? What a cow!"

Settling his brother in the car, Daniel said, "Stay out of bars in Rome, will you? It makes me nervous just to think of it. They have vendettas over there. That guy was right—your face is pretty, too pretty to be carved up.''

But Kyle had quietly passed out and didn't hear a word of his older brother's lecture. Daniel glanced at Kyle as he drove. He would have his hands full trying to take over Philton. Who was going to take care of Kyle? Between them, Daniel and his father had always made sure Kyle stayed out of trouble. Now it was Daniel's job alone.

God, he thought wearily, he missed his father already. Theirs had never been a sentimental relationship, but his father had always been there, quietly watching over everything. His death had left a giant gap in Daniel's world. He didn't even know if work would be able to fill the hole....

Daniel shrugged his shoulders wearily. Right now he couldn't even remember if he had successfully taken his father's place.

Why couldn't he remember? Daniel thought in frustration. In eleven years, so much would have changed. Who could he call? Who could he trust not to send him back? He had to be careful. If the nightmare was any indication of what it was like for him at Greenleigh, he would never go back. He couldn't take a chance on calling the wrong person.

Clenching his fists, he swung away from the window. He caught her off guard and the look in her eyes surprised him. It was a deep sadness, a shocking loneliness.

"You never told me what you had planned to do for the two years you were going to have charge of Danny."

He paused suddenly. Even he was beginning to think of Danny as another person, or maybe a youthful doppelgänger was a better way to put it. It was a weird, weird feeling.

Shaking his head, he continued. "Surely you weren't planning on staying hidden all that time."

She shrugged. "I didn't think that far ahead. I just wanted to get you out. I was prepared to do whatever was necessary for the future."

"That's it," he said suddenly. "That's what I can't figure. Why? Why on earth would you be prepared to do all this? You would have been giving up two years of your life...and for what?"

For Danny's happiness, she answered silently, and for her own happiness. How could she explain that to him? He had been skeptical of everything she had told him. How could she add that she was in love with the man he used to be, the man he was yesterday? She could hear him sneer, "In love with an idiot?" She shivered. No, she couldn't ever tell him why she had done it.

"You need to eat," she said, making her voice sound matter-of-fact. "We can't even think about what to do until we get food inside us."

As Daniel watched her working in the small kitchen area, he found himself fascinated by the way she moved. Why was he so drawn to her? She turned suddenly, and he felt a shaft of desire pierce him; the sensation was so strong it was overwhelming.

He had to regain control of his emotions, he thought, frowning. It wasn't like him to be obsessed with a woman, or anything for that matter. His control and his use of logic had always been his greatest strengths. He couldn't allow that to change now.

"It's chilly," he said, standing abruptly. "I'll get wood for the fireplace while you're finishing." Without waiting for a reply he walked out.

He found neatly split logs in a wooden shed not far from the cabin, but didn't attempt to take them in at once. He needed time to think.

A little way from the cabin he sat on a decomposing log and stared around him. He didn't know what part of Nevada they were in. Hell, he only had her word they were in Nevada at all. They could be in Alaska for all he knew, he thought, throwing down in disgust a stick he held.

Daniel had never felt so useless. He had always been the one to take charge. He was the mover, the doer. He got things done. Now he was as helpless as the six-year-old she told him he was yesterday.

Not for long, he vowed silently. As soon as he got back his strength and his memory, he would end this situation. And once more he would be the man in charge.

Amanda listened to the silence, feeling relaxed for the first time that day. But then, this was the first time today that she had been alone, without those watching eyes. He was driving her crazy. She didn't know how much more she could take.

He had been gone for fifteen minutes, too long to get wood, she thought. Maybe he needed to get away from her as much as she needed to get away from him.

The original odd couple, she thought wryly, then laughed and the sound surprised her.

Later, she was to remember that laughter wistfully. The second he walked back into the cabin carrying an armload of wood, all serenity fled. Throughout their silent meal and as she cleaned up afterward, she felt the heat of his gaze on her, following her every movement until she felt she would scream if he didn't stop.

Finally, she had had enough. Laying down the dish towel, she turned slowly to face him.

"I think I'll take a walk," she said tightly. "I need some fresh air." And some space, she added silently. Turnabout was fair play.

She hadn't gone three steps into the woods when she found him beside her. She closed her eyes briefly. He probably thought she was going to try to leave. She almost laughed aloud. Where would she go? She couldn't go far enough or fast enough to forget it was all her fault. No, she thought, whatever happened next, she was in this situation for the duration.

They walked in silence, and even though he was no longer watching her, the silence was different from what she had experienced with Danny. It wasn't comfortable; it wasn't companionable.

Gradually she began to take in the beauty of the woods, and it calmed her. Spring was just reaching the low-lying mountain area, and green was bursting from every tree and bush. Flowers of pink and white were just beginning to open.

Suddenly, on the path ahead, she saw a tiny blue butterfly, its wings fluttering in azure joy. Exclaiming, she turned to the man beside her. "Oh, look—isn't it beautiful?"

Pulling his eyes away from hers, he stared after the butterfly. After a moment, he nodded, then glanced up at the trees above them.

Amanda swallowed her disappointment. He wasn't Danny. She would have to tell herself that over and over until she knew it by heart. By heart, she repeated silently. That was painfully funny—her heart was the only part of her that knew for sure that this man wasn't Danny.

She stared with something close to resentment at Daniel's upturned face. Suddenly, he swayed. Perspiration sprung out on his forehead. When he staggered, she lunged at him, wrapping her arms around his waist.

"What is it?" she asked, the blood pounding in her veins. "What's wrong?"

"Just help me get back to the cabin," he said shortly, as though he resented having to ask for her help.

Please, God, let him be all right, she begged silently as they made their way slowly back to the cabin. Each step became a major accomplishment as he grew heavier and heavier.

Panting, she pulled his arm around her shoulders. "Just keep it there and hang on," she said, her voice rough with determination. "A few more steps. A few more steps." The words became a litany, a prayer for survival. The whole time they struggled forward, she thought, I can't do this, as her heart pounded painfully in her chest.

She almost cried in relief when she saw the cabin through the trees. "We made it," she gasped, her eyes stinging with perspiration. "We really made it."

Pushing open the door of the cabin, she staggered with him to the bed. When he fell awkwardly across it, she leaned over him, wiping his face with the sheet.

"What can I do?" she asked anxiously.

"It's going away," Daniel said. "Don't fuss."

Gradually his lie became truth as the dizziness diminished. After a while, he glanced at the woman still leaning over him.

She's terrified, he thought in amazement as he studied her features.

Daniel was completely baffled. He didn't know what to think about this small woman. What was her angle? She certainly didn't look mercenary right now. His gaze drifted over her. In fact, she looked beautiful. Too beautiful for her own good. Too damn beautiful for his own good.

Shifting on the bed, he tried to sit up, but when he moved, the room swam crazily. He shook his head stubbornly when she tried to help. He had to do it alone. By sheer force of will, he physically pulled himself into an upright position.

He sat quietly, watching her move reluctantly away from the bed, watching as she refilled the lanterns and poked at the coals in the fireplace. He knew she wanted to discuss what had happened out in the woods, but he refused. He hated the weakness that had gripped him; he hated the way it brought back the fear, fear that what she had told him about the mysterious disease was the truth.

As the day slowly passed, the charged atmosphere between them grew stronger, building to unbearable proportions. Amanda was almost relieved to see the sun go down. At least she could ignore him in her sleep. Opening the cedar chest, she took out more blankets and began to prepare the couch.

"I'll take the couch," he said suddenly.

Amanda glanced up. "But—"

"You sleep on the bed," he said, cutting her off sharply. "I'll take the couch."

"That doesn't make any sense," she protested. "You're too tall for the couch."

Pulling the cover from her hands, he acted as though she hadn't spoken and silently began to spread out the sheet and blanket.

He was obviously used to having his own way, she thought later as she changed in the bathroom. Staring at her face in the mirror, she frowned. Had it been only two days since they had left Greenleigh? It seemed impossible. It felt lifetimes ago.

Turning around slowly, she leaned against the sink. How long before he fell asleep? How long before she felt safe from those piercing eyes? Sighing, she moved to sit on the edge of the bathtub to wait.

Daniel lay perfectly still, listening to the soft sound of her slippers on the wooden floor. With eyes barely open, he watched as she walked to each lantern, blowing them out in turn. Then she moved to the bed and dropped the robe to a chair.

Moonlight struck her body, making her gown invisible, exposing the shadowed, secret places.

He closed his eyes, stifling a groan. He had lain there for hours thinking of her. Now the desire burned through him, consuming him, until he wanted to scream in frustration.

Moving silently, she climbed into bed. He heard her body sink into it and imagined her dark hair spreading out across the pillow. What would it feel like to touch it? What would her skin feel like, taste like? Her scent was elusive and beckoning, driving him mad.

What had happened between them the night before? he wondered, not for the first time. Had he touched her, loved her? He was almost willing to give up the eleven years if he could just remember last night.

She shifted restlessly, and he felt every muscle contract in response. This was crazy, he thought suddenly, his lips tightening. Why shouldn't he make love to her? They were married—he had the paper to prove it. It was his conjugal right. Maybe it would get her out of his system. Maybe sanity would return.

Shadows brushed by the soft touch of moonlight didn't hide the sudden stiffening of her body beneath the blanket as he approached the bed. Suddenly she rolled over and stared up at him, her eyes wide in the darkness.

"We're married," he said harshly as he threw back the covers and lay down beside her.

Pulling her into his arms, he felt her trembling beneath his touch, but it didn't matter. All that mattered was that she was here next to him, and she belonged to him. She *belonged* to him. With feverish movements, he pulled the gown off and almost groaned at the warm, soft beauty of her.

With shaking hands, he touched her hungrily, exploring all the places he had seen in his imagination. But no amount of imagining could equal the reality. She was lovely beyond words, beyond thought. Bending his head, he tasted her, reveling in her, marveling at the softness of her skin. His eyes closed tightly as he let the feeling penetrate his flesh, filling every corner of his mind.

He ran his hands over the rounded curves, exploring them, branding them with his touch. When his fingers sought the dark, curling triangle between her legs, she moaned, making his pulse pound crazily, spurring him on.

"Please, no," she whispered urgently, pain evident in her voice. "Oh, God, you're not Danny."

Daniel stiffened. Instantly he felt the desire ebb away, leaving him drained of emotion. He lay still for a moment. Suddenly he felt a rush of violent jealousy for the man called Danny, even though logic told him that he and Danny were one and the same.

Rising slowly from the bed, he stared down at her. "You win," he said, his voice cold. "I won't touch you again."

Later as he lay wide awake on the couch, he heard her crying, softly and helplessly. Strangely, he wanted to comfort her. He rolled over and pressed the pillow to his ears, blocking out the sound.

Chapter Twelve

Amanda put the last pan into the soapy water. From the corners of her eyes, she looked at the man standing beside her, drying the dishes as she handed them to him. They were both being very careful not to mention what had taken place the night before, each pretending that it had never happened.

"There's something soothing about doing dishes," he said, his voice thoughtful as he reached up to put a bowl away in the cabinet. "Someone should patent it."

She laughed, then stopped suddenly, surprise showing on her expressive face as she stared at him.

"I may not be Danny, but I am human," he said in exasperation.

She tensed immediately and, angry with himself, he snapped at her. "For heaven's sake, stop watching me constantly for symptoms."

He threw down the dish towel and turned away, running a hand through his hair. "This is crazy. We can't sit around here waiting for each other to fall apart."

Pacing a few steps away, he moved his shoulders wearily. "If only I had some of that drug. We could at least check to see what it is." Daniel had felt the dizziness again that morning, and it bothered him more than he cared to admit. "Then maybe I could go to a local doctor for this treatment you say I need so desperately."

She swung around and stared at him, her eyes hopeful. "Do you really mean that?"

He shrugged. "What difference does it make? You said I destroyed all you had."

Reaching into the pocket of her slacks, she pulled out a small glass vial. "I found it when I was cleaning up the glass. It had rolled under the bureau." She glanced away suddenly, avoiding his eyes. "I was saving it, in case..." Her voice drifted away.

"In case I freak out again?" he said, his voice dry. "Don't look so damn guilty. It may happen yet."

He took the glass vial from her, holding it gingerly between thumb and forefinger as he stared down at it. Then he raised his eyes to hers. "All right, let's go find civilization and see what we can do."

Amanda vaguely remembered the town of Allendale, twenty miles to the north of the cabin, but they needed the help of her road map to reach it. While

Allendale was not exactly a thriving metropolis, it was picturesque in a rough-hewn sort of way and contained all the necessities. At certain times of the year, she remembered, the town attracted its share of tourists. Luckily for them, early spring was not one of those times.

"Do you know a doctor here?" he asked as they drove through the main section of town.

She stared ahead, her eyes thoughtful. "I didn't come to the cabin often when Mom and Dad had it. There was one man my parents mentioned occasionally... Beidermyer, yes, that's it, Dr. Beidermyer. He and Dad played poker together, and he was the one who took care of Mother's asthma attack." She glanced at Daniel. "I've never met him though. I don't even know if he's still here."

He pulled the convertible to a stop next to a telephone booth. "I can find out real quick."

Seconds later he came back to the car. "He's still listed," he said, glancing down at her. "I assume there is only one Beidermyer allowed to a town," he added dryly, then nodded toward a gas station. "Since it's a route number, I'll have to ask them for directions."

Amanda saw him approach the blue-uniformed attendant. Then amazingly, as he stood talking to the man, Daniel began to laugh. She had never seen him laugh, and it shocked her. It made her wonder what he would be like under normal circumstances.

How would she react if she woke to find eleven years of her life missing? she wondered to herself suddenly. She had been so absorbed with the fact that he wasn't Danny, she had shut out the fact that he was a man under extreme pressure.

When he returned to the car, all evidence of the laughter was gone and, unreasonably, she felt a pang of loss.

"The doctor retired last year," he said as he slid behind the wheel, "but apparently he still helps out in an emergency. Hal says he lives about a mile west of town."

"Hal?"

"The attendant," he said, then fell silent as he concentrated on the road.

End of conversation, she thought, envying Hal as she glanced away from him.

The doctor's house wasn't difficult to locate. It matched perfectly the description, which Daniel had repeated to her, offered by the station attendant. Painted blue and white, the gingerbread-style house was neat as a pin. Somehow it added normalcy to their quest.

The door opened at the first knock to reveal a man with thinning white hair. The lines of good humor that radiated from his pale-blue eyes and the slightly bulbous nose would have made him look jolly had he not been so tall.

"Dr. Beidermyer?" Amanda said. When he nodded, she said, "We've never met, but you know my parents—Jed and Donna Timbers? I'm Amanda, and this is Daniel Phillips. We'd like to talk to you if you have time."

"Of course," he said, pleasure showing in his eyes. "Come in, come in."

When they were seated in a small, comfortable study and had refused his offer of refreshment, the doctor said, "How are Jed and Donna? I get a card from them occasionally, but not nearly often enough. The last one was from France."

She nodded. "They loved France. Ireland is home base for them, but I don't think they stay there very often. They've always wanted to travel, and now that Dad is retired, they just don't stop."

The older man laughed. "That sounds like Jed. He's a whirlwind. Donna always seemed a little stunned by him."

"Dr. Beidermyer," Daniel said, and Amanda could sense his impatience. "We've come to you for some advice, and it's a little...frankly it's a little sensitive."

"Shoot," the doctor said. "Even though I've retired, I'm still a licensed physician and, as such, will respect any confidences given me."

Daniel nodded, relaxing visibly. "I appreciate that."

When he smiled, Amanda's eyes widened. The smile was as stunning as his laugh.

"The problem is my teenage nephew," Daniel said. "For a few days recently he stayed with us at Amanda's cabin and left some things behind. When we were boxing them up to send them on to him, we found this." He pulled the vial out of his pocket. "On the whole, he's not a bad kid, and I don't want to upset his parents unnecessarily. Can you tell us what it is?"

Amanda wondered if her mouth was hanging open. He had told the fabrication so easily. No one could have guessed that it was not the absolute truth.

Dr. Beidermyer took the vial from Daniel while he fumbled in the breast pocket of his shirt for his glasses. "I can certainly try," he said, studying the label. After a moment, he glanced up. "I'm afraid I don't recognize the name, but that doesn't mean anything. It could be the manufacturer's rather than a generic name. Or it might even be fake." He pulled off his glasses, frowning slightly. "I could send it to the lab in Las Vegas to be analyzed."

"How long would that take?" Daniel asked.

The older man rubbed his chin. "If I put a rush on it, I could have the results back in two, maybe three days."

Daniel nodded. "That's fine. We'll take care of any charge, of course."

Later in the car, as they drove back to town, Daniel held his silence, but somehow she sensed a change. Just outside the city limits, he pulled the car over to the side of the road. Resting his chin on the steering wheel, he stared straight ahead.

Amanda could feel the tension in him. She jumped skittishly when he slapped the steering wheel with his open hand.

"There's nothing we can do until we get the results from the laboratory. Agreed?"

She nodded slowly, wondering at the intensity in his voice.

"I can't stand the thought of going back to that cabin right now. There's nothing to do there but think." He turned his head toward her. "And I've had enough thinking to last me two lifetimes. So how about a truce? A vacation from this hell?" There was an underlying urgency in him that couldn't be disguised. "Why don't we have lunch, then do some sight-seeing like two ordinary tourists who have nothing more pressing to think about than if they have enough film in their camera."

Before she could answer one way or the other, he turned his head and met her gaze. "Look, I know this thing has been eating at you, too. We both need a day off."

She closed her eyes. "That sounds like heaven. Absolute heaven."

"Well, I don't know about heaven," he said, smiling slowly. "But then I never figured I would make it to heaven anyway."

For lunch, they found a small café with genuine Nevada artifacts decorating the walls. Afterward, as they walked around the small town, Amanda felt three hundred years younger than she had that morning. It was a strange sensation, watching his personality unfold. At first the change was hesitant, then it seemed to come with a rush of relief.

They played Mom and Pop Tourist, pointing out things to each other like the post office and the VFW lodge. There were times when she would realize with a sense of shock that this laughing man beside her was the same man who had practically accused her of marrying him for his money. But every time a negative thought appeared, she shoved it down again, determined to make the most of this small gap in reality.

"And this is, of course, the pride of Allendale," Daniel said as they walked along the cracked sidewalk.

She glanced skeptically at the mud-brown, three-story hotel he indicated. "Yes, I can see that." Then she leaned toward him and whispered, "Why is it the pride of Allendale?"

"Are you kidding? Haven't you heard of all the famous people who have slept there?"

She shook her head. "You're not going to tell me that George Washington slept there, are you? Because I don't believe it."

"George Washington?" he repeated, raising a brow. "Small potatoes, my dear Amanda. We're talking about people like Fats Domino and Troy Donahue."

She threw back her head and laughed. They had really and truly called a truce. Neither of them made any reference to the past or even the uncertainties of the present. It was as though they had agreed to pretend to be someone other than who they really were. If they also had to pretend to be at ease with each other, then it was working beautifully. Amanda had somehow separated in her mind the man she was with today, not only from Danny, but from the cold stranger in the cabin.

"Oh, there's a drugstore," she said, pulling on his arm. "Wait here for me while I get some toothpaste."

Without waiting for a response, she ran across the street and entered the drugstore. The small store reminded her of movies she had seen about the fifties. There was a soda fountain on one side of the room with shiny, stainless-steel equipment behind the counter and swiveling stools in front of it.

Toilet and health items crowded the walls and one center display and it took her a few minutes to find the toothpaste. She grabbed a bottle of aspirin on her way to the cash register at the back of the store.

As she dug in her purse to pay for her purchases, she heard someone move behind her and glanced around.

"Daniel," she said in surprise. "I'm sorry. Was I taking too long?"

He stared at her for a moment in silence, then smiled and shook his head. "I decided I couldn't miss seeing the drugstore. When you finish, I'll buy you a Coke," he added, nodding at the soda fountain.

There had been a strange quality to his smile, something she couldn't put her finger on. But she didn't dwell on it. Today wasn't the day for dwelling, she decided as she moved to join him at the counter.

Later, as he drove, Daniel whistled under his breath. Even now, when they were on their way back to the cabin, she was aware that the atmosphere between them had undergone a subtle change, and she couldn't put her finger on exactly what the change was.

It was only as she was climbing into bed that night that it occurred to her that she could have gotten in touch with Ted while they were in town.

That was why he had followed her into the drugstore. He had been testing her and evidently she had passed. Without realizing it, she had placed their destinies in his hands.

The next few days should have been tense ones, but strangely they weren't. It was as though each recognized the fact that there was nothing they could do for the time being except wait.

For Amanda it was a time out of time. As she sat on the rug in front of the fireplace with Daniel beside her, she thought of how strange it was that they should have been here only four days. Time had both expanded and contracted.

She smiled, remembering her physics professor. He had tried so hard to get her to grasp the fact that time had no independent existence apart from the order of events by which humans choose to measure it. He would be pleased to know that she finally understood. Without the darkness of night to show the passing of the time, the past few days would have been a single experience.

Every day, Daniel was remembering more about the missing eleven years. There were still large gaps, but they knew now that it would just take time.

Even though his returning memory pleased them both and the tension had eased, living with him was still not a comfortable experience. Exciting and unfathomable, but never anything so mundane as comfortable.

At times he would be abrupt, even cold. Never once had he apologized—at least not in words, she amended. Every time he was short with her, every time his temper flared, he would do some small thing for her to show that he regretted his behavior.

What bothered her more than his abruptness was something that was going on inside herself. She had tried to tell herself it was due to being cooped up in a small space with him. But deep down she didn't believe it and her reactions worried her. Because Amanda had finally admitted to herself that she was physically attracted to Daniel and had been from the beginning.

It seemed wrong; she wasn't even sure if she liked him. Why was she suddenly wondering what it would be like to be kissed by him? To be touched by him?

Always before, when she had been attracted to a man—even Danny—the mental and emotional attraction had come first. The physical part was simply an extension of the other.

She even wondered if she was feeling something similar to what Virgie felt, but she knew she wasn't. Virgie needed sex for sex's sake, the man didn't matter. As Amanda glanced at the man sitting beside her on the rug, she knew that she wouldn't feel this deep need for anyone except Daniel.

"Okay, let's start again," he said, startling her out of her reverie, bringing a slight touch of color to her cheeks. "Where were we?"

"You were telling me about something that had happened at Christmas," she said. "Was that before or after your father died?"

"Before," he said after a moment of thought. "I remember Lena worrying because he was so late."

She had learned from their talks that Lena was his stepmother and Kyle, his half brother. Daniel's own mother had died before he had had a chance to know her.

"She shouldn't have worried," he continued. "Dad was always late. He loved that company. Philton was his life. For a while after he died, I felt like a usurper every time I walked into his office and sat in his chair."

"How was your relationship with Lena?" she asked. She had found that asking him about the times before the eleven-year gap sometimes awakened one of the lost memories.

Daniel stared into the fire, recalling the face that was sweet and pretty but lacking strength. "We got along fairly well. She was very pretty and lots of fun to be around."

"Did you notice that you said 'was'?"

"She died," he said suddenly. "Two years after Dad."

"I'm sorry. No one should have to lose two mothers in one lifetime."

"She was never my mother." He said the words, not resentfully but matter-of-factly. He could recall vividly the day his father had brought Lena home as his new wife. Daniel had been a very shy five-year-old, and in the space of one day his whole life had changed.

"Daniel, we have a surprise for you." His father turned to the small blond woman standing beside him. "Lena and I were married this morning. What do you think of that?"

Daniel's green eyes were solemn in his thin face as he stared up at Lena, studying her, gauging her reaction to him. Then she smiled, and the room lit up.

"Well, Daniel," she said, "do you think it will work? Do you think I'm mother material?"

She wanted to like him, and she wanted him to like her. Daniel could tell by the way the smile reached her eyes. He held his knees stiff as they began to tremble slightly.

He extended his hand toward her. "I'm glad it's you," he said, his small-boy voice husky.

Ignoring his hand, she enveloped him in a hug that smelled of flowers and sunshine. "So am I, honey."

No, Lena had not been his mother, but she had been a friend. And without her, Daniel wouldn't have had Kyle. Kyle had changed the texture of his life. Suddenly there was a vibrant new voice in the house, filling the empty spaces, dispersing the loneliness.

When they had brought him home from the hospital wrapped in a blue blanket, Kyle had been red and squalling and demanding. But to seven-year-old Daniel, it hadn't mattered that the baby was ugly. Kyle was special. Daniel felt it when he looked at his brother, and he saw his opinion confirmed in Lena's and his father's expressions. Kyle was special....

Daniel felt very important as he walked into the sitting room. Lena was reading and didn't hear him enter. He looked down at the paper in his hand. His essay had been chosen as the best in the whole sixth grade. He himself would read it to the school on Friday at assembly.

"Lena," he said, his voice filled with quiet intensity.

She glanced up from her book. "Daniel," she said in smiling surprise. "Is it time for you to be home already?" She studied his face. "You look like you're about to explode. What's this?" She reached for the paper he held.

Before she could do more than glance at it, they head a wail from the hall. Together they rushed out of the room. Kyle's chubby face was red and streaked with tears as he sat on the stairs, rubbing his leg.

Lena scooped him up and sat down with him in her arms while Daniel hovered anxiously. "What happened, darling?"

"Dan left his truck on the stairs and...and I tripped," he sobbed.

"Daniel," Lena said sternly. "That's not like you. You're usually so neat."

Daniel frowned. Kyle must have forgotten that Daniel had given him the truck to play with that very morning. "I'm sorry, Lena," he muttered. "I won't do it again. I'm sorry you got hurt, Kyle."

"It's all right," Kyle said, his tears dissolving in an engaging chuckle. "You always find my toys for me. I guess this time I found one for you."

Daniel and Lena laughed, neither of them noticing the crumpled essay that lay on the polished wood floor.

"Lena was a good woman," Daniel said, still staring into the fire. "But somehow I always felt like a spare tire. I saw her face when she was with Kyle—" his eyes took on a faraway look "—and I knew I was missing something." He shook his head and laughed. "It wasn't her fault. Kyle was chubby and cute and always laughing. I was not exactly a cuddly sort of kid."

Though Amanda was sure he hadn't intended it, Daniel's words painted a too-vivid picture of his childhood. Suddenly Amanda felt angry for the child he had been all those years ago, always yearning for warmth and love but not knowing how to get it. She could imagine him solemn and quiet, but always wishing he could be different.

Daniel watched Amanda from the corners of his eyes, wondering what she was thinking. These memory sessions couldn't be very interesting for her, but she always asked another question, as though more were involved than just his remembering, as though she were working out a puzzle.

"Lena didn't marry again after your father died?" she asked.

He shook his head. "Two years isn't that long. She was very much in love with my father. I'll always be grateful to her for that."

Lena's death had been harder on Kyle than it had been on Daniel, even though the younger man hadn't been with her at the end as Daniel had. Kyle had flown back from Italy for the funeral, and the change in him had shocked Daniel. The change hadn't been only physical and mental; it had been emotional as well.

"I need a drink," Kyle said as they left the cemetery together. They had not talked about Lena's last hours yet, and Daniel wondered if Kyle would be able to handle it.

"You look like you need about a month's rest," Daniel said. "What have you been doing to yourself over there?"

Kyle grinned. "You know what they say about Italian women."

"If your dissipation is due to Italian women, I think you'd better come home and stick to good old American girls."

"I wouldn't, even if I could," Kyle said, his voice unexpectedly solemn. "I'm making a life for myself over there, Dan. You wouldn't believe the people I do business with. Powerful men, men who can have anything in the world they want just by snapping their fingers."

Daniel studied his brother silently. "Are you working too hard, Kyle? Is the business worrying you?"

"Hello, no." Kyle glanced up at Daniel. "This is a switch. I never thought you would tell me to stop working."

"You can carry anything too far. Just don't overdo it. And for heaven's sake, let me hear from you once in a while. It shouldn't take a tragedy to get us together."

Kyle fell silent, and Daniel knew he was thinking of Lena. He would never tell his brother how she had begged for her son at the end. Daniel could spare him that pain. . . .

Daniel frowned. Italy was a long way away, but that didn't explain why Kyle had not been to Greenleigh in the whole time Daniel was there. Surely someone had told him when Daniel was institutionalized.

"How old were you when you were married?"

Daniel's thoughts came back to the woman beside him with a jolt. It took him a second to assimilate her question, then he grimaced. "Nineteen, if you can believe that," he said, giving a short laugh. "Not even dry behind the ears."

Daniel didn't like to think about his marriage. It had lasted only six months, but he always felt he should have known what was happening sooner. Her name was Joanne—pretty, sweet, greedy Joanne.

"But Daniel, everyone will be at the Baxters' tonight. We've just got to go."

He watched Joanne silently as she stood naked, pulling dress after dress from the closet. He tried to call up the emotions he had felt when he had married her, but even desire was gone.

"I told you last week I won't go to this party," he said quietly. "You're free to go by yourself."

She swung around to face him, her features unattractive with mottled anger. "You're jealous," she hissed. "You know Stu Baxter likes me, and it's eating away at you."

"Don't be coy, Jo. Everyone knows you're sleeping with Stuart Baxter." He turned his back on her, the sight of her making him a little sick. "I just wish you had decided you liked the fun-loving type before you married me."

"You bastard," she spat out. "Do you think I intended it to be forever? Stu's lawyers are working on the divorce papers right now."

She bit her lip, and Daniel knew she had told him more than she had intended. He smiled. "I'm afraid you're a little late, my darling wife. My lawyer beat you to it."

Her face was bright red with fury. "On what grounds? I warn you, you won't get away with telling lies about me, Daniel. If you make trouble...if you don't give me everything that's coming to me, I'll tell everyone the truth."

"The truth won't hurt me, Jo," he said wearily. "But I have a feeling the truth isn't what you have in mind."

"It's the truth all right. You haven't touched me in two months. And I know why." Her voice was smug. "You don't like women, do you, Daniel. I'll bet Stu could hire a private detective and get pictures that would shock everyone in California."

Daniel smiled. "People in California aren't so easily shocked. Don't even try it, Jo. You'll make a nice sum for having put up with me for all these months. I advise you to be satisfied with that."

But she hadn't, of course, Daniel thought. He glanced at Amanda. "I deserved everything I got. It taught me a lesson. I learned real quick that she was more interested in being Mrs. Daniel Phillips than in being my wife. Dad bought me out of that one, but I made sure he never had to do it again."

Amanda turned away from him, afraid to let him see what was in her eyes. It all fit together, she thought. At last she understood why he seemed so hard. The lesson he had learned was to trust no one but himself.

Sitting up straighter, she said, "Tell me again about Philton. Surely someone who worked there eleven years ago is still there."

"Jonas Brady?" he murmured. He thought of the lined face of the man who had been his right hand and his father's before him. Then he slowly shook his head. "It doesn't make any difference. Even if Jonas is still there, I wouldn't get in touch with him. I wouldn't even call Kyle."

She stared at him in bewilderment. "Why not?"

"I've tried to look at this from the other side. Everyone I know surely has heard that I was institutionalized. If I call and say, 'Hey, I'm all right now,' what are they going to do? If they cared at all, they wouldn't take a chance that I was wrong. They would feel it was their duty to try to get me back to Greenleigh. And I don't think I could stand it." Again he shook his head, but more emphatically this time. "No, even if I knew of someone I could trust, it wouldn't be fair to put that kind of burden on anyone." He stretched. "I guess I'll just have to confront the dragon by myself."

She stiffened in shock. "Why do you say that?"

He glanced at her in inquiry. "I just explained why. I don't want—"

"No, no," she said, shaking her head. "Why did you phrase it that way—'confront the dragon?'"

His eyes were puzzled. "I don't know. It just came out that way. You look strange. Why does it matter how I put it?"

She blinked back unexpected tears. "It doesn't matter," she assured him huskily. "It just seemed a little out of character."

He smiled wryly. "If that means you can't picture me in a fantasy, then you're right. I'll leave the fantasies to you."

"And what is that supposed to mean?" she asked, anger effectively drying her tears.

"You're the Don Quixote around here, not me." He paused for a moment, studying her. "But you're not really, are you? I think I've finally figured you out."

"Oh, really. How nice for you," she said, her voice heavy with sarcasm.

"Yes, really. You were in love with him, weren't you?"

The words were said bluntly, startling her as they fell into the heavy silence. Jerking her head around, she avoided his eyes. He knew too much. It was none of his business.

"Weren't you, Amanda?" This time the question was soft, almost sympathetic.

She shrugged, still looking into the fire. "What does it matter now? He's gone."

He leaned forward, poking the fire distractedly. "He was me...if that's grammatical. But I guess even if it's not, he was still me. I was he." The silence drew out, then suddenly he said, "Tell me about him."

"Daniel—" she began.

"No, I mean it. I want to know about him. You seem to think he was someone special.... I can tell by the way your eyes go soft when you remember him."

She swung her head around to look at him. He had said practically the same thing about the way Lena looked at Kyle. She was almost sure he hadn't made the connection, but it didn't matter. She had, and it was enough for her to swallow her hesitation.

"Danny was very special," she said, confirming his earlier statement. "Danny found miracles. There are not many people who can do that. He also accepted people as they are. Not many people do that, either. He never judged or resented; he just accepted." She swallowed heavily. "All my life I've been positive that if anyone saw the real me, the one that is sometimes black, sometimes gray, but never spotless white, they would be put off. So I've always pretended—not a big pretense. Just enough to make people think I'm nicer and kinder and smarter than I really am. Danny knew that sometimes I'm thoughtless and sometimes I'm selfish, and he accepted it. He did more than that," she whispered huskily. "He loved me, faults and all."

The silence drew out as she remained caught up in her memories of those days at Greenleigh. She was startled out of her reverie by a knock at the door.

Jerking her head up, she glanced at Daniel. Although his expression didn't show it, she knew he was just as shocked as she was. It seemed wrong somehow that another person existed. Until now, theirs had been an exclusive world.

When she opened the door she found Dr. Beidermyer on the porch. "The results came in this morning," he said without preamble. "I'm afraid they don't tell us much." He handed Daniel a sheet of paper. "The lab broke down the chemical composition, but they couldn't say what they do when combined. If it's any help, there is no known mind- or mood-altering drug listed there."

After glancing at the paper, Daniel handed it to Amanda. She stared at it for a moment, but it was imcomprehensible to her. She might as well have been trying to read the Rosetta stone.

"You didn't have to make a special trip," Daniel was saying. "We were going to come into town tomorrow."

"No special trip," the doctor assured him. "A friend of mine lives about seven miles past here. I come up about once a month, and Jerry and I see how outrageous we can act. Being this far from civilization does something to you, doesn't it?"

Amanda watched Daniel as he talked casually with the older man. She had never been able to read his emotions in his face, and now was no exception. But she knew how she was feeling. They had pinned all their hopes on this analysis only to find it told them absolutely nothing about his condition.

As the doctor turned to leave, he said, "I did have another idea, but I wasn't sure if you wanted to pursue this thing."

Daniel was instantly alert. "I'd like to find out any information if possible," he said casually.

The doctor nodded. "Well, I have a friend in Tucson—he's in research with a pharmaceutical company—and he's as close to a genius as I've ever met. He's got one of those freak minds that remember everything. If this stuff is anything more than a random mixture of ingredients, he'll know about it. Of course, it may take a while," he warned.

"I can wait," Daniel said, and Amanda heard the determination in his voice.

When the door closed behind Dr. Beidermyer, she turned to him. "Daniel," she said, hesitantly. "I'm sorry."

He shrugged. "We're not any worse off than we were yesterday. We still know nothing."

She didn't understand. He actually seemed undisturbed by the news. As she stared in bewilderment, he reached out and touched her face. "It will be all right, Amanda. Don't worry so much."

At his touch, she felt a wave of sensuality so strong that it made her dizzy. A lightning-quick pang of disloyalty struck her. Then she reminded herself that Danny was gone. He was like time. He didn't exist outside her memory of him. At last she accepted what she had fought for days. Danny was a sweet dream. Daniel was hard, strong reality.

Chapter Thirteen

Oh, Daniel, look!"

Daniel leaned against an oak tree and watched Amanda. As she knelt to touch a small white flower he felt desire shoot through his body.

It was a reaction that he should have gotten used to by now because it happened every time he looked at her—no, it happened every time he thought of her. Since, in his thoughts, he was free to do what he wanted with her, the nights had become pure, unadulterated hell.

He couldn't ever remember wanting a woman the way he wanted Amanda. He was becoming obsessed by her. The need to touch her at times pushed every other thought out of his mind. Other than the months he had spent in Greenleigh, most of his past had come back to him, but even the desperation he had once felt to recover those eleven years diminished beside his hunger for this small woman.

Sometimes he wondered how she could spend every minute of every day with him and not feel the intensity of his desire. To him, it shouted; it screamed. But she acted as though he were some damn eunuch.

Only that morning, as he had leaned over her to wake her, she had looked up at him with beautiful, sleep-glazed eyes and murmured, "Danny."

Daniel had wanted to shake her until her teeth rattled. He had wanted to scream obscenities at her. At times, although he didn't like to admit it even to himself, he found himself wishing he could be Danny, that poor unfinished creature that she cared about so much.

He had to stop thinking about her, he told himself as a frown twisted his lips. He had enough problems without adding her to the list. He had learned a long time ago that the only thing in life he could count on was himself. That hadn't changed.

As he watched, Amanda raised her face to the sun, closing her eyes as the rays warmed her, and Daniel felt every resolution and every ounce of logic disappear. She looked like an ancient pagan goddess giving silent tribute to the sun god . . . and at that moment he knew that no amount of silent arguing, no amount of reason, was going to make him stop desiring her.

His lips curved upward in a grim smile. No man is above acting like a fool, he told himself ruefully.

"Are you going to stand there all day?" she called to him over her shoulder. "I thought you were going to gather some kindling."

When he didn't answer immediately, she stood, her eyes concerned. "Are you feeling all right?"

He pushed away from the tree and said, "You weren't supposed to ask that question again, remember?" When she bit her lip, he said lightly, "I'm fine, and if I have to say it again, I will be genuinely, thoroughly ill. Then you can fuss over me to your heart's content. But until then—stifle it."

She laughed, her blue eyes sparkling as she went back to picking flowers. He had, after the first couple of days, refused to talk to her about the illness he was supposed to have. He wasn't willing to deal in vague possibilities, only in realities. Reality was what he could see for himself. Other than the loss of the six months he had spent in Greenleigh, he was fine. No, he would deal with this mysterious illness when and if it presented itself to him.

"You look like you're contemplating the great mysteries of life," Amanda said as she walked toward him carrying an armful of flowers.

"How did you guess?" he said, smiling. "Deep, profound mysteries...like why you never see really beautiful women on commercials about constipation or hemorrhoids."

She laughed. "That's profound all right. But the answer's not so tough. Beautiful women are never constipated and never get hemorrhoids. Or dandruff or the heartbreak of psoriasis...and I can't believe we're having this conversation. Are you having television-withdrawal symptoms?"

"Never in this lifetime," he said dryly. "But now that I think about it, a movie wouldn't be bad. I wonder what's showing in Allendale."

She glanced at him skeptically. "Didn't you see the sign last time we were in town? It apparently takes a while for movies to get to this part of Nevada. I think last week it was *Abbot and Costello Meet Frankenstein*."

"Abbot and Costello are vastly underrated," he said, frowning at her in disapproval. "Abbot had a genius for timing, while Costello was the perfect *homme d'esprit*."

"Who?" she asked, wrinkling her nose.

"Who's on first," he said, deadpan.

While the movie they saw that afternoon was not quite as old as the one Amanda had mentioned, it was one that had already been on television in L.A.

Nevertheless, Amanda enjoyed every minute of it. For once, Daniel seemed almost carefree. They ate popcorn dripping with butter and slightly stale chocolate-covered raisins and spoke in whispers, ripping apart the movie's plot, its actors and its corny dialogue. They smothered laughter behind butter-coated fingers.

As they drove away from the theater, she was struck by the gleam in his eyes. Suddenly he turned into the parking lot of the grocery store.

He turned to her, resting his arm on the steering wheel. "I've just had the most brilliant idea."

She laughed, shaking her head ruefully. "Do you expect me to be impressed? The last brilliant idea you had was the prewar epic we've just seen. Need I say more? I think the record speaks for itself."

"Steaks," he said, making the word sound important. "We've been living out of cans for days now because of that contrary refrigerator. Why don't we pick up a couple of steaks and cook them on the grill?"

She stared at him for a moment. "Okay, I'll admit it—I'm impressed. Let's go."

In the small store, they not only bought the best steaks in the house and the trimmings to go with them, they also picked up a carton of the biggest, most beautiful strawberries she had ever seen.

"I can't believe you got whipped cream," she said as they placed the groceries in the back seat. "That's almost sacrilegious. No sugar, no cream—I don't think I'll even wash them before I eat them."

"God, you're drooling," he said in disgust. "Remind me to stay out of your way when—"

Daniel broke off abruptly when they heard her name being called. Glancing around, Amanda saw Dr. Beidermyer stepping from his car.

"Amanda, Mr. Phillips," he said when he reached them. "You've saved me a trip."

"Did you hear from you friend in Tucson?" Amanda asked, excitement entering her voice.

The older man shook his head. "No, there's no word yet. I was just wondering about your nephew," he explained, glancing at Daniel in inquiry. "I don't suppose he lives around here, does he?"

"My nephew? No, I'm afraid not," Daniel said, frowning. "Why did you want to see him?"

"Is the boy one of those science nuts?" The doctor took off his glasses and began wiping them with a blue handkerchief. "Kids nowadays amaze me. They build computers and atomic bombs in their basements with mail-order science kits. They'll be fiddling around with DNA before you know it, if they haven't started already."

"What was it you wanted to know about my nephew?" Daniel prompted.

"I don't know if Jed told you, Amanda," he said, turning to her, "but I play around at research. I've got a small lab behind the house. Nothing elaborate—a microscope, some test tubes and white rats"

"No—no, he didn't tell me." Her eyes were alert as she stared at the older man.

"Well," he continued, "I only sent a small sample to Tucson, and so I decided while we were waiting that I might as well test what I had left on my rats . . . just to see what would happen, you understand."

"What happened?" Amanda and Daniel spoke at the same time.

"It was the damnedest thing," he said, shaking his head. "I'm thinking seriously about writing a paper on it. This is going to interest a lot of people."

"Dr. Beidermyer, what happened to the rats?" Amanda asked, unable to keep the urgency out of her voice.

"What . . . oh, yes. They started to regress immediately," he said. "It was the most interesting thing I've ever witnessed. Mature rats tried to suckle a female as though they were newborn." He scratched his head, his eyes thoughtful as he continued. "The period of regression lasts only as long as the drug is administered. I can't tell you exactly what happens, but apparently the drug isolates and numbs the memory portion of the brain, so that adult knowledge is subdued, leaving the juvenile identity in control."

As he spoke, he seemed unaware of the shock waves rippling through the two people beside him. "I haven't tried it yet," he said, "but I assume that increasing the dosage would numb all memory."

"What would happen then?" Amanda asked, the words a barely audible whisper.

"The regression would be complete. The rat would go back to the fetal stage."

"Which means?" Daniel asked, his voice harsh, his face rigid.

"It means that the heart and lungs would eventually stop functioning—death."

Chapter Fourteen

I've talked to a friend in Las Vegas," Dr. Beider-myer continued, unaware of the bomb he had dropped, "and we're going to try to duplicate the stuff. But I sure would like to talk to your nephew to get the exact ratio of ingredients." He laughed. "I can't wait to see what brain-wave patterns the rats give off during their regression."

Amanda stared at Daniel, forgetting Dr. Beider-myer completely. Her head was swimming. It was too much to take in all at once.

As quickly as they could, they made excuses for themselves and Daniel's nonexistent nephew. The drive back to the cabin was interminable. Amanda could almost feel the hostility in Daniel, and she understood it. He had been deliberately drugged. Ted

Sutherland had kept him a prisoner, and he identified her with Greenleigh.

Suddenly she gasped. He turned to look at her. "They died," she whispered in horror. "All the people taking the drug died." She pressed a trembling hand to her mouth, her eyes wide with fear. "And I was going to give it to *you*. If you hadn't destroyed it—" She was shaking all over. "If—"

He pulled the car over and took her by the shoulders, giving her a hard shake. "Stop it, Amanda. It doesn't do any good to blame yourself."

"Why not?" she said, laughing hysterically. "You are."

He didn't deny it. He didn't respond at all. He simply pulled the car back into the narrow road and continued driving.

One of the bags in the back seat shifted and she remembered, as though it had happened in another lifetime, the plans they had made for the evening. Their laughter, their earlier companionship, mocked her. That was before he decided she had conspired against him.

As soon as they were inside the cabin, Amanda turned to him. "We've got to talk about this," she said tightly.

"I need to think," he said, turning away from her. "We'll talk later."

She grabbed his arm. "You never want to talk when it's important!" she shouted, tension exploding in anger. "You watch me and watch me until I want to scream, but you never talk. Goddamn it, we've got to get this settled. This place is driving me crazy. You're driving me crazy!''

It was the spur Daniel had been waiting for. All the tension of the past few days came to a head. Grasping her, he jerked her hard against him. He cupped the back of her neck, pulling her mouth to his, bruising her, making her feel his anger.

After a stunned moment, Amanda shoved away from him, staggering back to put a trembling hand to her lips. Flushed, tears of anger on her lashes, she rasped out, "You said you wouldn't touch me again."

"No, I'm not supposed to touch, am I?" he ground out. "All that's for your sweet Danny." His blazing green gaze drifted over her in contempt. "It suited you to have him a little off, didn't it?"

She backed away as he stepped closer, her eyes wide as she listened. "What are you saying?" she whispered.

He stared at her silently for a moment, then slowly he said. "How was your sex life, Amanda?" His voice was cold and hard. "What was it like with Danny boy?"

She closed her eyes tightly against the assault, silently begging him to stop. He made it sound sick, obscene.

"No, look at me," he said, grabbing her shoulders to shake her. "A strong, mentally healthy man doesn't suit you, does it? That's too threatening. You have to take too many chances . . . because you're no longer in control."

"Stop," she whispered hoarsely. "You don't know . . . you're wrong." She closed her eyes briefly, then opened them to stare up at him. "You could never in a million years understand what I had with Danny. You're cold." She backed away from him toward the door. "You're cold and dead inside." Swinging around, she ran out of the cabin.

Amanda didn't even know where she was going; she simply knew she had to get away from him. Branches and brambles pulled at her clothing, tearing them as she ran, but she ignored them. Her breath came in harsh gasps as she tried to escape him, to escape his lies.

Then she heard Daniel behind her, and suddenly he caught her arm, swinging her around violently, jerking her body against his.

She fought like a wild thing, sobbing as she struck out at him blindly. But he didn't release her. When he tripped on an exposed root, he rolled with her in his arms until he was lying on top of her.

"Cold," he ground out, his eyes furious slits. "Am I cold, Amanda?" he asked as he pushed her cotton blouse up over her breasts. Burying his face in the soft flesh, he said, "Am I dead?"

Amanda brought her hand up to tear at his face, but he caught it roughly in his, folding it down to her side. There was anger in his every movement. He punished her breasts, sucking at them, pulling at the nipples with his teeth, building a hated fire in her loins. She moaned against it; she moaned for it.

Then as abruptly as it had begun, the assault stopped. He didn't remove his body from hers, but neither did he touch her.

For a long time, she lay there with her eyes closed, listening to the harsh sound of their breathing, then slowly, she opened her eyes to look at him.

He was staring down at her and this time his expression was easy to read. The anger was gone, disappeared like a bad genie sent back to the lamp. In its place was the most anguished yearning she had ever seen.

"Daniel?" she said, her voice husky.

His hand was shaking as he reached up to touch her cheek. "How can you think that I blame you for what happened?" he whispered harshly. "Don't you think I know that without you I would still be there?"

But Amanda didn't want to hear about blame or Greenleigh or even about the harsh words that had just passed between them. She didn't want to remember who she was or who he was or that they were poles apart in every way. He had built a fire in her that prevented her from thinking at all.

Meeting his gaze, she held it as she raised her head slowly. She was so close she could feel his breath on her mouth. She moved slightly and touched her tongue to his full lower lip.

The groan that came from deep in his throat shook her to the core. It reverberated in the air, sending erotic messages to the secret parts of her, the womanly parts of her. The emotion that surged between them was charged, not with anger but with a desperate hunger. No longer was she fighting against him; she was fighting for him, for his touch. She was struggling for his lips.

The fingers that had tried to claw at his face now clawed at his clothing. When they were naked, when she felt his hard, heated flesh against hers, there was a sweet savagery between them. The tensions and anger of the past made the present all the more urgent.

Tremors shook her as he cupped her buttocks in his large hands and entered her at last. "Daniel...oh, Daniel," she heard someone moan, then realized the voice, so husky, so filled with desire, was hers.

Their slick, overheated bodies merged into one beneath the canopy of trees. She writhed against him, meeting every urgent thrust with an urgency of her own. Time stopped as her one desire in life became Daniel. The pressure, the agonizing need, built until she thought she would scream for it to stop...or go on forever.

Violent shudders had just began to wrack his body when the climax of their mating exploded inside her, touching every part of her, leaving her changed.

She knew she would never be the same person again. A blindfold had been lifted from her eyes. Here, in the grass with this man, she had collided with life. She had met it head on, and now she knew the wildness of it; now she knew the savage beauty of it.

When the tremors stopped at last, she felt the cool air on her bare flesh and closed her eyes briefly as reality began to return.

What had happened to her? she wondered in desperate confusion. What had brought about this unasked-for change? This wasn't the gentle loving she had had with Danny. This was love on the edge.

She closed her eyes in embarrassment, remembering the way she had pleaded for his touch, remembering the urgency with which she had touched him.

Without looking at the man who lay next to her, she stood and began pulling on her clothes. After a moment, she heard him rise to his feet to do the same, but still she didn't look at him. She was too confused, too unsure of herself.

When he touched her arm, she flinched violently.

"Amanda—" his voice was strange, almost gentle "—now I think we had better talk."

She nodded and walked away from him. At the cabin, they sat at the table across from each other. Amanda stared down at her hands in silence. Tension was gone, but wariness had taken its place.

"You said Sutherland had developed this 'treatment.'"

His voice startled her, so involved was she in her own thoughts. She was relieved that he wasn't going to bring up what had happened between them in the woods. She wanted to erase it from her mind.

Feeling his gaze on her, she nodded, responding to his question. "I still can't believe it," she said, her voice subdued, her eyes worried. "I know he has to be the one who did that to you, but I just can't take it in. He's a world-famous physician and researcher. What possible reason could he have for doing that to you? Surely he wasn't experimenting on human beings?"

"I don't imagine he did it on his own," Daniel said. "I assume someone paid him to do it."

Amanda glanced at him in surprise. She hadn't considered that possibility. Money inspired people in some very ugly ways. "Maribel Fortnoy," she whispered suddenly.

"Who?"

"She was one of the Special Ones…like you. It was her death that made me realize you were going to die, too. She had a terrible niece who inherited everything upon her death, millions and millions of dollars."

He looked up, his eyes narrow. "So it would have been worth quite a sum to get rid of her in an unsuspicious way."

She glanced at him hesitantly. "Who inherits your money?"

Smiling grimly, he said, "That was the first thing I thought of. But it doesn't work. Kyle inherits it. Even if by some wild stretch of the imagination I were willing to consider my own brother a suspect, he doesn't need the money. When my father died, we inherited equal shares of his estate. If anything he's better off than I am…at least right now. The Italian end is going great, but most of my capital, my disposable assets, are tied up because of a takeover fight. At least they were the last I remember."

He stood and ran a hand through his hair. "I need to know what's going on at Philton right now. Tomorrow I'll call Jonas. I should have called him days ago," he muttered, almost to himself. "He still keeps up with the company and should be able to tell me what's happening. He might even be able to tell me who is responsible for my being at Greenleigh." He paused, then added, "I don't have to tell him where I am."

She nodded, closing her eyes. She was tired, too tired to think anymore. She felt she had lived ten years today. Without warning, she sensed movement and jerked her eyes open, watching warily as he stood and walked around the table.

"We can't do anything tonight. Try to put it out of your mind. You've had a rough day," he said softly, reaching out to stroke her hair.

Amanda stiffened, unable to take her eyes from him.

"You hate me," he murmured, and she could detect no regret in his voice. "And you probably hate yourself as well. But it doesn't matter. The same thing is going on inside you that's going on inside me. And you can't deny it. You need me as much as I need you."

Stooping, he lifted her in his arms and carried her to the bed.

Amanda wanted to argue. She wanted to scream that he was wrong. But he wasn't wrong. She needed him. She was dying for him.

Chapter Fifteen

Daniel pulled the convertible over to the side of the street and drifted to a stop in front of a telephone booth. Tension filled him, overflowing until he felt it touching the woman beside him. He should have left her behind at the cabin, but he knew without asking that she wouldn't have stayed.

He stared for a moment at the booth, his mouth settling into a grim line. Slowly, he shifted his shoulders, forcing himself to relax before he stepped from the car without a word to Amanda.

Jonas would tell him what he needed to know. If there was a man on earth he could trust besides Kyle it was Jonas Brady.

* * *

"You've got to stay, Jonas." Daniel leaned forward, placing his forearms on the desk that separated him from the older man. His father's desk. "At least for a little while. Just until I get things going."

Jonas's brown eyes had turned almost amber with age. In one hand he held an ancient pipe and used it to scratch the bridge of his nose thoughtfully. "I don't know, Daniel. I only stayed because your father seemed to expect it of me. Now that he's gone, it just doesn't seem like the same place."

Daniel glanced down at his hands for a moment, then he said quietly, "This place needs you, Jonas. I can handle the work, but it's going to be a while before everyone accepts me. That'll happen a lot sooner and a lot easier if I've got you backing me. Everyone trusts you. You and my father built Philton."

Jonas studied him in silence. "Are you planning on changing things? You know what they say about new brooms."

Daniel hesitated, then he met the older man's eyes. "I'm not going to lie to you. There will be changes. I have ideas I've been sitting on for years. But I'll never make a change simply to show I'm boss. I won't change anything that doesn't need changing. When I'm positive—absolutely positive—that my way is better, then I'll make the change." He paused. "I want you here, Jonas. But if you can't live with what I'm going to do, then I'll accept your resignation."

It was several minutes before the older man spoke again. "You've got a lot of your father in you, but there's a lot that's just you."

"Does that bother you?"

Jonas stood and held out his hand. "As a matter of fact, I think I like it. We'll work well together, Daniel."

And they had, Daniel thought as he stepped inside the booth. Picking up the telephone, he slipped a coin into the slot. Even though he was retired, Jonas would be able to tell him what was happening at Philton. He was a good man, a trustworthy man. But still Daniel wouldn't tell him where they were. The naked singularity.

"Jonas?" he said when the phone was picked up on the other end.

"Yes? Who is this?"

"Jonas, it's Daniel."

"Daniel?" The old man's voice quavered. "Where are you? Are you all right? What in hell has been going on?"

"I'm fine, Jonas," Daniel said. "Whatever was wrong with me before is gone. I'm back on track."

"Yes," the old man said slowly. "Yes, I can hear it." Now there was deep satisfaction in his voice. "By God, I knew nothing would keep you down. You're too much your old man's son. This is great, Daniel. Just great."

Daniel hesitated but only for a moment. "Jonas, I need some information."

"Shoot. I'll tell you what I can."

Shifting his stance, Daniel leaned against the wall. "Who took over when I . . . while I was away?"

"Beeker," Jonas said immediately. "He seemed like the logical choice to everyone concerned. Was that all right?"

Daniel pictured the short, sturdy man. He had been with the company for years and had taken Jonas's place as Daniel's right hand. No, Edgar Beeker wasn't responsible for this, Daniel thought, frowning.

"Beeker was fine," Daniel said. "Jonas, tell me everything that happened when it was discovered that I was ill."

He heard the old man exhale heavily. "It all happened so fast, Daniel. We had lunch on Wednesday as usual . . . do you remember that?"

"No, I'm afraid my memory is a little fuzzy. I remember that we have always had lunch together on Wednesday, but I'm afraid I can't recall that particular Wednesday."

"Well, you were fine. Your usual self. You told me you had to go to some kind of fund-raiser that night. All the bigwigs in California were supposed to be there. The next morning—that was Thursday—I got a call from your secretary. Everyone at Philton was in a panic. I had a job making them keep their mouths shut. If word had gotten out that you were sick before a successor could be chosen, Philton's stock would have dropped out of sight. Anyway, it seems that you had some kind of attack at the fund-raiser and had been taken to the hospital. Just happens that Dr. Sutherland was at the dinner, too. He rode with you to the hospital, and when your own doctor couldn't be located, he examined you and recommended that you be moved to his place. I forget the name of it."

"Greenleigh Acres?"

"Yes, that's it. I didn't care for the idea because you know my doctor won't let me travel that far. But your doctor backed him up and when they talked Kyle into the idea, too, there was nothing I could do about it."

Daniel straightened away from the wall of the phone booth. "Kyle? Kyle was here?"

"He flew in a couple of days after you were hospitalized. He wanted to take you back to Italy with him, but the doctors and board members convinced him you would get better care from Sutherland. He stayed until you were settled in at Sutherland's place, then flew back to Rome."

"Jonas, this is important," Daniel said, gripping the telephone tightly. "Do you remember which of the board members wanted me at Greenleigh?"

"Eventually all of them," he said, his voice puzzled.

"But in the beginning, who pushed for it?"

"Couldn't tell you, Daniel. I was getting most of my information secondhand. They called me in to calm things down, but I barely got to talk to anyone in charge, not even Kyle. By the time I did, the decision had already been made." There was a long pause. "You think there was something funny going on at Sutherland's place?"

The old man was still sharp, Daniel thought, smiling grimly. "I can't say yet, Jonas. There are still a lot of things to work out."

Actually, it was only one thing, he told himself, one very important fact. Who did this to him and why? Who wanted him out of the way so badly they would pay someone to kill him?

In the car, Amanda stared at the phone booth, watching Daniel's face, studying it intently as he talked. How could they have been so close last night and so far apart this morning? she wondered in confusion. When they were making love he became a different person. He opened himself up to her; he was generous and warm and loving. But the rest of the time there was a solid wall between them, a wall of his making. Had he ever allowed anyone to get close to him? It had suddenly occurred to her that even when he laughed with her, he was pretending. He was hiding behind an effective facade.

Yet, despite the wall, something had grown between them. Amanda knew it couldn't even be described as a love affair; it was more of a mutual obsession. The attraction between them—the sensual ties—was stronger than anything she had ever felt.

Shifting restlessly, she wondered just exactly what she was looking for from him. Why did she keep demanding, to herself, that there be more? Anyone would think she actually wanted him to be in love with her.

Suddenly she closed her eyes weakly. Was that what she wanted? Was she in love with Daniel?

She couldn't answer the question. Their relationship was too complicated to be summed up in such a simple phrase. Even if she finally decided that she loved him, it didn't change the fact that he was a man who would never allow himself to love in return.

She closed her eyes for a moment. Just for a moment, she allowed herself to think of Danny. But crazily, she couldn't summon up his image. In her mind, he had somehow merged with Daniel.

Just then, Daniel stepped out of the booth and walked toward the car. She pulled herself upright.

"You're pleased," she said quietly as she examined his strong features.

"Kyle's home," he said. "Jonas just told me he's staying at the house. When he found out I was missing, he dropped everything and flew over from Rome."

"Daniel, that's wonderful. Will he help?"

"He's my brother," he said simply, then he pushed a hand through his hair. "We've got problems I hadn't thought of. Jonas says there's a full-scale manhunt underway. The police are looking for us everywhere."

She drew in a sharp breath. "Does that include the Nevada police, too?"

"According to Jonas, it includes every police department in the country... and the FBI."

"Oh, my God," she whispered. "They think I kidnapped you, don't they?"

He cupped her chin in his hand and lifted it, meeting her eyes. "Don't worry," he said softly. "I'm here, remember. They won't catch us, but even if they did, I wouldn't let anything happen to you. I give you my word on that."

Amanda wanted to believe him, but she knew if the police found them, they would arrest her first and ask questions later. It could take days to get it straightened out.

"Amanda," he said firmly. "I said I would take care of you. I don't give my word lightly."

She exhaled slowly. "No...no of course you don't. I'm not worried, really. It's just a little strange to think my face might be on post-office walls all over the country." She grinned suddenly. "I'm torn between hoping it's not the picture from my driver's license and hoping it is. If it is, no one could possibly recognize me from it. On the other hand, if I have to gain notoriety, I like to do it looking my best."

He threw back his head and laughed in genuine amusement and Amanda felt as though clouds had lifted and the day had grown brighter.

"Did Jonas tell you anything?" she asked, shading her eyes with her hand as she looked up at him.

He shook his head. "Nothing substantial. I know who took over after I left, but it doesn't mean anything. Ed Beeker isn't a man after power...and that's what this is all about. I'm sure of it. There are a lot of ambitious men at Philton, men who would break a few rules to get to the top." He frowned thoughtfully. "The thing about power is that the need for it grows in direct proportion to the amount attained—the more you get, the more you want. When people get in the way, sometimes it's necessary to run over them."

"That sounds so cold," she said, shivering slightly. "I don't think I could live in that world, always wondering if one of my associates is out to get me."

He shrugged. "You get used to it. And after a while it gets to be a game . . . king of the hill."

She shook her head, then met his eyes. "What do we do now?"

He drew in a deep breath. "Now we call Kyle." Turning away, he walked back to the booth.

"Kyle?" he said a few seconds later.

There was tense silence on the other end, then Kyle whispered, "Dan? God, Dan, is that really you?"

Daniel laughed. "Yes, it's me. Listen, Kyle, and don't say anything until I'm through."

This time Daniel left nothing out. He told his brother everything he knew about what had happened to him, everything that he and Amanda had pieced together.

Five minutes later, Kyle let out a long breath. "Son of a bitch," he said roughly. "I can't believe it. It's like a science-fiction movie. But you're really all right...I can tell by your voice. You can't imagine what it was like knowing that physically you were Dan, but mentally you were—"

Kyle broke off and laughed harshly. "I can't take it all in. It's just so incredible. When are you coming home?" His voice was urgent. "I want to be with you when you talk to the police about Sutherland...just in case they don't believe that you're really all right again." He swore viciously under his breath. "That bastard Sutherland. I always knew there was something phony about him, but I just thought it was that pretty-boy smile. I sure never thought of anything like this. Hell, I panicked like everyone else when I heard that nurse kidnapped you."

"She isn't a nurse," Daniel said, frowning. "She's a bookkeeper. And she didn't kidnap me. If it weren't

for her, I would still be in that place. I owe her a lot."
Like my life, he added silently.

"My, my," Kyle said. "What's this note I hear in your voice? Don't tell me you've been getting your kicks while we were all going crazy. Where are you anyway?"

"That doesn't matter." He was annoyed, and he didn't know why. Kyle was a casual devil, but Daniel didn't like him talking about Amanda as though she were a roll in the hay. "What's important is that I'm on my way home. It may take us a while; can you wait there at the house for us?"

"Do you even have to ask, brother? I won't set foot outside until you get here. But Dan, can't you tell me—"

"I've got to go now, Kyle. I'll tell you all about it when we get there."

He hung up and stepped out of the phone booth. His head was throbbing slightly, his pulse pounding. Fight or flight. Why should he react that way? It was almost finished now. He could hand it over to the police, and they would find out who had done this to him.

Shaking his head, he walked back to the car. "We'll have to drive to Los Angeles," he told her. "The police are probably watching the airports."

"When do you want to leave?"

"Now," he said abruptly, and slid behind the wheel.

It was the same trip she had made two weeks before, only this time they were driving the other way. Now she didn't feel that everything was on her shoulders. She didn't have to pretend to be strong.

Miles and miles of Interstate 15 roadside scenery passed by as Amanda watched silently, sometimes dozing, sometimes listening to the radio, but rarely talking. She could feel him getting more and more tense with every mile that brought them nearer to Los Angeles.

Daniel didn't even slow down until they reached Las Vegas. Amanda watched the city pass, thinking how different it seemed from the last time she had seen it.

That night, that terrifying night, seemed to have happened to someone else. All the fears she had had, all the doubts, were echoes now. She had lost Danny, but in losing him she had given him back his life.

There were lines of weariness around his eyes when Daniel pulled into the parking lot of a small diner on the western edge of the city. After they had given the waitress their orders, Amanda put her forearms on the Formica table and leaned toward him.

"What if the police can't make Ted tell who paid him? How are you going to be able to go back to work?"

His eyes narrowed and the look in them made her shiver. "I'll find out," he said quietly. "With or without Sutherland." He glanced up. "But I don't want to talk about it now. For just a little while, I want to forget about what's happened. Talk to me about things that happen in the normal world. Tell me why you decided to be a bookkeeper."

"I don't think I ever made a conscious decision . . . I mean I didn't spread a dozen careers out in front of me and say, 'I'll take this one.' Dad was a bookkeeper, and he took me to work with him occasionally.'' She shrugged. "It just always felt right.''

"Tell me about your childhood,'' he ordered.

She frowned. "Daniel, you don't really want to hear all this.''

"Yes. Yes, I do,'' he said firmly. "I want to hear about your Christmases and when you lost your front teeth. I want to hear what boy you had a crush on in the sixth grade.''

She felt strange, talking about such trivial things, and began hesitantly. But after a while, after she realized that he really did need to hear the things she was telling him, that it in some way soothed him, she began to relax.

"Then in the first grade, I met Mrs. Appleton,'' she said, smiling.

"You liked her,'' he said, studying her face.

They had eaten and were finishing their second cup of coffee.

"I liked her,'' she confirmed. "I still can't figure out why she didn't call my parents and complain about me. Before we ever met face to face, I had harassed her unmercifully.''

He raised one dark brow. "You?''

She laughed. "Me. I could be a brat at times. Instead of an ordinary doorbell, she had a real brass bell on her porch. It fascinated me. Every morning as I walked to school I would detour by her house just to ring her bell...then I would run." She shook her head. "She must have been over seventy then, and arthritis made her move very slowly. But old age had no reality to a six-year-old." She laughed softly. "Then one day, sitting on the porch under the bell, I found a cigar box full of crayons...and my name was printed on the top of the box."

He chuckled. "That was a slick move. I think I would have liked your Mrs. Appleton."

"You would have loved her. I did," she said, remembering. "I thought about the crayons all night, then the next afternoon—after school—I went back and rang the bell again. This time I waited. She asked me in just as though she had expected me. In all the time I knew her—she died when I was eighteen—she never once mentioned the bell or those crayons."

He stared at her for a moment. "I wish I had known you then."

She shook her head. "No, you don't."

"Why do you always underestimate yourself?" he asked. "Everyone has faults, but not everyone faces up to them the way you do. That takes real courage."

She laughed. "Now I know you're crazy. I don't have an ounce of courage. The night we left Greenleigh I was shaking so hard I could barely hold on to the steering wheel. I kept saying, 'I can't do this. I can't do this.'"

"But you did it," he said softly. "Courage isn't fearlessness. It's not giving in to the fear."

She glanced down at her cup in embarrassment. "I don't know about that," she said, then raised her eyes. "I—"

Suddenly she broke off, drawing in a sharp breath. "Daniel," she whispered, staring in horror at the doorway as two policemen walked into the diner.

"Don't panic," he said, taking in the situation at a single glance. "They're not looking for us. They're simply taking a coffee break." The two men had sat down at the counter and were now laughing and talking with the waitress. "We're leaving now, Amanda, but we're not in a hurry. We've simply finished our meal. Right?"

She nodded jerkily and stood when he did. Her legs felt like rubber and she couldn't understand how they could carry her all the way across the room. But they did, and minutes later she and Daniel were once more on their way to Los Angeles.

It was early in the morning when Daniel sat in a chair in a small motel room, watching Amanda as she slept. Her dark hair was spread out over the pillow. There had been no question of separate rooms when they had checked in. Maybe she didn't like what was between them, but she had accepted it.

The room was full of echoes, he thought as he leaned his head back. Echoes of their lovemaking. Echoes of the taste of her flesh, the feel of her body.

He stood and moved to the bed to stare down at her. Why did he get the panicky feeling, the fight-or-flight sensation, when he looked at her? Why, suddenly, did he want to turn around and go back to the cabin?

Chapter Sixteen

Amanda awoke slowly. She didn't open her eyes at once but merely lay there. She could feel Daniel's warmth beside her and wanted it to last a little while longer.

When she felt him move, she raised her eyelids reluctantly. His head was next to hers on the pillow, so near she could see the flecks of gray in his eyes. The look in those eyes burned through her, branding her with his heat.

She didn't even know him, she thought in amazement. She didn't know him, and yet they were bound inextricably.

He threaded his fingers through her hair, framing her face, never taking his eyes from hers. "In a few hours, we'll be in Los Angeles," he whispered huskily. "It will all be over." Moving his head, he brushed his lips across hers. "This time, don't make me feel like I'm taking something from you. Give it to me freely, Amanda. And just as freely, take what I have to give."

Again his lips found hers, and she closed her eyes, trying to absorb the feeling. There was urgency in the kiss, but only a hint of the desperation of the night before. That desperation had puzzled her, still puzzled her.

His lips moved to the corner of her mouth, then down to the nape of her neck. "Say yes, Amanda," he whispered against her throat, the words almost a moan.

"Yes," she said hoarsely, clutching his shoulders. "Yes and yes and yes."

Wrapping his arms around her, he crushed her body to his and she could feel his heart pounding. The taste of him, the feel of him, had consumed her for what seemed like forever. His hungry mouth on hers triggered a wildly explosive response. She clasped his neck, defying him to leave her, and met the warm moistness of his mouth with her tongue.

She heard and felt his gasp of surprise at her response, and then he groaned, an agonized sound, and pulled her beneath him in an exquisitely intimate, thoroughly possessive embrace.

Lifting his lips from hers, he sought the warm flesh of her throat. A quivering tension was building inside her and when he sought her breasts, teasing the tips with his tongue, she was breathing in frantic gasps. With closed eyes, he brought one hand up to cup the fullness, urging it closer to his mouth. His hands felt electrically charged, as though all the desire in him were concentrated in the tips of his fingers.

The pagan pleasure visible in his strong face was the most blatantly erotic thing she had ever seen. She clutched wildly at him, reveling in the feel of his hair-roughened chest and thighs pressing against her softness. She clung to him, arching her hips convulsively, entwining her legs with his as though she would pull him into her body.

A slick sheen of perspiration covered them both, brought by the frenzy of their writhing bodies. Clasping her buttocks with his large hands, he slid downward, pressing his face into her belly, trying to merge with her softness.

She caught her breath in a startled gasp as she felt his hot breath on the throbbing place between her thighs, becoming one with the inferno he had already built there.

Sounds penetrated her pleasure-drugged mind. Husky, animal sounds. Somehow she realized that the sounds came from her own throat.

The feeling of being completely immersed in tactile sensation was mind-numbing, absorbing her completely. She moved her hand over his thigh, exhaling a soft, moaning breath when she found his pulsating strength.

The effect on Daniel was explosive. He moved swiftly, powerfully, and suddenly she was beneath him, feeling the hard length of his body against the eager softness of hers. His mouth devoured hers frantically, his tongue plunging deep into the seductive depths of her mouth.

He entered her with a desperation that told her it could be no other way. The fiery sweetness filled her, taking her to a different, more basic level. Nothing mattered except that she reach that special place. The place she could reach only with Daniel.

Then suddenly, with overpowering strength, he took her there and their tightly clasped bodies shuddered together in prolonged ecstasy.

When the world stopped whirling around her, Amanda opened her eyes and glanced at him. His eyes remained closed, but as though he sensed her gaze on him, he whispered huskily, "Amanda, I've never— I can't explain it. It's the most incredible thing I've ever experienced in my life."

"I know," she said softly. And she did. She knew just exactly what he meant. What happened between them when they made love was beyond explanation. The future was a closed book and she had no way of knowing what would happen for the rest of her life. One thing she was sure of—this thing between them was a once-in-a-lifetime thing. It was something she would never experience with another man, because it could only happen between the two of them.

Two hours later, in a booth in the café attached to the motel, they sat across the table from each other, as far as the world was concerned an ordinary couple. Again their relationship had undergone a subtle change. Daniel had allowed her to get a glimpse of the man he really was.

"Would you or your wife like orange juice, sir?" the waitress asked, staring at her pad.

When she left, Daniel glanced across at Amanda, a strange gleam in his green eyes. "Do we look so much like an old married couple? Surely the honeymoon couldn't be over after only two weeks."

Amanda drew in a sharp breath. How could she have forgotten she was married to this man? But as incredible as it seemed, she had. Even in Las Vegas, when memories of the night they were married were so strong, she hadn't connected those memories to Daniel. With all the turmoil, with all the revelations of the past two weeks, she had simply overlooked it. Or had she purposely put it from her mind?

"What's wrong?" he asked, some of the stiffness returning to his voice.

She shook her head helplessly. "I didn't foresee any of this happening when I took us to that chapel in Las Vegas." She ran her finger around the rim of the water glass, staring at it with intense concentration. Inhaling deeply, she glanced up. "I suppose since you weren't responsible for your actions, the marriage is void. It should be easy to get an annulment, don't you think?"

He glanced away from her and it was impossible to tell what he was thinking. After a moment he met her eyes. "It might have been easy in the beginning, but I'm afraid I wasn't mentally incapacitated when we made love this morning . . . or last night or the night before." His smile was slightly mocking. "That might make a difference."

Amanda clenched her fists in her lap. Did he regret having made love to her? she wondered as she stared at his stony features. As usual, she found no clue there. But she couldn't believe he regretted it. The sensations had been too strong to be one-sided.

When their breakfasts arrived, they both merely sat pushing the food around on the plates. With one swift movement, Daniel pushed his aside and stood. "Let's go," he said abruptly.

One step forward and three steps back, she thought as she stared out the window of the car. What did he want from her? At times she thought she caught glimpses of the lonely boy he must have been, but then before she could be sure, he shut her out, pushing her away violently. She was beginning to think that no mortal would ever truly know Daniel Phillips; no one would know the person he was beneath the rock-hard facade.

It was early afternoon when they reached Los Angeles at last, and the traffic, as always, was frantic. Once they were in the city, Amanda lost track of the turns they made. She only knew for sure that they eventually came to a hilly section where elaborately landscaped mansions lined the streets.

Suddenly, Daniel made a U-turn and drove in the opposite direction. "What's wrong?" she asked in concern.

"I need time to think," he said stiffly as he pulled the car over to the side of the street and parked. "Kyle will want to call the police as soon as we get to the house."

She nodded in confusion. "Of course he will. I thought that was what you wanted. He'll be able to confirm that you're all right."

He was broodingly silent for a long time, then he said, "All afternoon I've been thinking about the men who work for me. I said there were some who were after power, but what I didn't say was that regardless of their ambition or lack of it, I only have men I respect working for me." He glanced at her. "I was so taken up with discovering who it was and having him put away that I didn't stop to really think. The reality is finally hitting me. One of those men...one of the men I respect tried to kill me." He raked his fingers through his hair. "I don't know if I want to know who did it."

She felt her heart swell with compassion. "Daniel," she said softly. "I know it's not going to be easy. But it's got to be done. You can't think about what you want now. You can only think about what's right. Ted Sutherland and the man who paid him have to be stopped—that's the bottom line."

With his arms wrapped around the steering wheel, he leaned his forehead against it. Then he inhaled slowly and leaned back in the seat. "Yes, I know it. I guess I just needed to hear it said aloud." He glanced at her. "Are you ready for the final act?"

"As ready as I'll ever be," she said, her smile slightly wry.

They covered the same ground they had covered before, and glancing at Daniel, she found his face rigid and knew they were getting close. Now that it was finally over, he should be relieved. But she knew he was anticipating the final scene with the police and was bracing himself to show no emotion. Emotion still wasn't allowed, she thought sadly.

When he pulled over to the side of the street and parked, she glanced around. She tried to see through the trees to the house beyond, but they were too thick.

"Is this it?" she asked quietly.

"It's a block down, across the street." Intercepting her questioning glance, he said, "The police may be watching the house."

She nodded and stepped from the car when he did. There was no question of her staying behind. It was as though he had finally accepted the fact that she was in it until the very end.

They had gone not quite a block, when he put his arm around her waist and bent his head close, as though they were engaged in a conversation. His eyes were trained on something she couldn't see.

"What is it?" she whispered.

He jerked his head slightly toward the end of the block. A black-and-white patrol car was headed toward them. Amanda stiffened automatically.

"Just keep walking," he said calmly.

As soon as the police car passed them, Daniel stopped and turned slightly, watching it swing into a driveway.

"Your house?" she asked.

He nodded. "I want to get closer, but we'll have to be careful. I haven't come this far to be grabbed at the last minute by the police."

"I don't really understand," she said as they crossed the street. "I know I don't relish having to explain why

I kidnapped you from Greenleigh, but surely you're going to the police to tell them about Ted?''

"Oh, I'm definitely going to the police, but only after I've contacted the district attorney. The word is out that I'm nuts. I'll just bet that Sutherland has convinced the police that it's urgent that he be the first one to see me . . . so he can give me my 'medication,' of course."

She stumbled slightly as the thought shook her. "You're right," she whispered hoarsely. "That's just what he would do. Then you would be in no shape to tell anyone anything."

"No," he murmured, staring down at her. "Because then I would be Danny."

For a moment she simply stared in confusion. Why was he looking at her like that? Before she could even react, he took her arm in a bruising grip and led her to a flowering bush, which hid them but gave them a clear view of the house. It was white and modern and elegant, with clean lines and no pretense. Daniel stared at it as though it were a place he had heard about but had never seen.

"My father built it for my mother," he said softly. "It's strange, but I feel as though I don't belong here anymore. It's not the kind of house I would choose. I just stayed here because it wasn't important enough to move. I think I'd like a house on the beach—something simple, something that really feels like a home."

Amanda had the feeling he had forgotten her presence entirely and even the presence of the policemen. The police car had stopped in the curving driveway, and now two policemen emerged. Before they reached the front entrance, the door opened and a man stepped out to meet them.

When she felt Daniel stiffen beside her, she moved to get a better look at the man, but he stood in the shadow of a large palm. He seemed to be discussing something with the policemen, but they were too far away for their words to be heard. After a few minutes, the two policemen returned to their waiting car.

Amanda followed it with her eyes as it turned onto the street and went in the opposite direction from which it had come. After a moment, she turned back to look at the house. The man was standing in the center of the dive, staring at the street.

When he turned his head in their direction, Amanda caught her breath sharply.

"That's Kyle," Daniel said quietly, moving away from the bush.

Reaching out, she caught at his arm. "No, wait," she said urgently.

He turned back to stare at her. "What's wrong?"

"He's wrong," she said, nodding toward the man in the driveway, the man with an artful curl on his forehead and strange, pale eyebrows.

Chapter Seventeen

W hat are you talking about?"

Amanda bit her lip at the terse question. The closed expression was on his face once more. Somehow she got the idea he was bracing himself for pain.

"I've seen him before," she blurted out. "I was under a bridge at Greenleigh looking for a . . . well, it doesn't matter what I was looking for. I was hidden, and I heard him talking to Ted about a patient. I thought there was something familiar about him, but I couldn't place him. I remember that just after that I started thinking about you, but I just didn't connect it. I mean, you don't look that much alike, do you?" she asked anxiously.

He didn't respond at once, but a look she had never seen before came into his eyes as he passed one hand over his face.

Oh, God, she thought. Please don't let him be disillusioned again. "Maybe it doesn't mean anything," she said, disbelieving her own words as she clasped his arm in both hands. "Maybe he flew in and out so quickly he only had time for a short meeting with the doctor to find out how you were doing."

He glanced at her, his face hard. "He came all the way from Italy and didn't have time to see me?"

"No, but wait, Daniel," she said urgently, feeling the tenseness of his muscles beneath her fingers. "There could be an explanation for that. When I first met you...I didn't want to know you." With her eyes, she begged him to understand. "I was uncomfortable because of your condition. Some people are like that. Maybe he wanted to remember you the way you were."

He inhaled slowly, roughly. "We'll just have to find out, won't we?"

When he moved into the trees to the side of the property, she followed helplessly. The backyard was open with a huge swimming pool directly in the center. Daniel walked across the patio, skirting umbrellaed tables and wrought-iron chairs.

She didn't catch him until he had reached one of the back doors. "Wait, Daniel," she whispered urgently, pulling at his arm. He turned slightly to look down at her. "What are you going to do when you get inside? Do you think he'll just say, 'Hi, Daniel, and by the way I'm the one who paid Sutherland'? He can deny the whole thing and...and—" her lip quivered "—what if Ted's in there? They could do it to you again."

He stared at her for a moment, then shook his head as if to clear it. "I can handle Kyle. I know when Kyle's lying. I could always tell. He could fool Lena all the time and Dad some of the time, but he could never fool me."

Twisting the knob, he began to push the door open.

"And Ted?" she asked. "Can you handle him, too?"

The fire that flared in his eyes before he turned back to open the door scared her. He didn't care if Ted was inside. In fact, now she knew he wanted him to be there.

Then he stopped, pulling the door toward him until it was open only a crack.

Beside him, Amanda saw through the curtains why he had stopped. Inside she could hear a phone ringing, and Kyle strode toward it. If he looked in their direction he wouldn't have been able to miss them, but Daniel didn't back away. He stood where he was and listened.

"Sutherland, damn it, where are your men?" Kyle said angrily. "You said they would be here by now. I have no idea when Dan will show up. Yes, yes, all the servants have gone." He paused. "That's easy for you to say. You aren't taking a chance on being here alone with him. I want someone here and I want them now."

Again he paused to listen, and this time he picked up a cushion and hurled it across the room in anger. Amanda glanced at Daniel, almost afraid to see his face. But there was no pain there; it looked completely void of emotion. It hurt her more than she ever could have imagined.

"Yes," Kyle said tightly after a moment. "Yes, I understand. Wait...what are you going to do with the girl...no, never mind. I don't want to know. Just be sure you take care of her. And remember that your hide is up for grabs the same as mine."

Kyle had just replaced the phone when Daniel pushed open the door and walked in.

The younger man swung around sharply, and a multitude of expressions played across his face. The first and most easily recognized was fear.

"Dan! You old son of a bitch. Where did you spring from?" he said, running a shaking hand across his brow. He moved toward Daniel, then something in his brother's face stopped him.

"What's wrong?" he said, glancing from Daniel to Amanda uneasily.

"That's what we'd like to know," Daniel said quietly. "Who was on the phone, Kyle?"

Kyle glanced at the phone, wetting his lips nervously. "Nothing important," he said, laughing. "I can never get away from business. But that doesn't matter. Are you going to tell me why you walked in here looking like the face of doom?"

Daniel shrugged his shoulders as though they ached. Then he turned away and walked to the window. "I know what you did, Kyle," he said wearily. "Now I simply want to know why."

"I don't know what—"

Daniel swung around to face him. "Amanda witnessed one of your meetings with Sutherland at Greenleigh."

Kyle's gaze slid over Amanda as she stood silently by the door. "And you believe her? You really are crazy. She must really be something to get you to turn on your own brother."

For a split second, Daniel's green eyes flamed, his nostrils flaring. Then the fire burned off, leaving coldly banked anger. "I heard your phone call, Kyle. Every word. You can't pretend anymore."

Kyle shoved his hands into his pockets. "I told you—I didn't do anything." His gaze skittered around the room, resting on everything except his brother. "You're sick, Dan. Dr. Sutherland says you've gone into remission. But I worry about this attitude of yours. It may be a symptom of—"

"Why, Kyle?"

The younger man turned his back on them and strode a few paces away, his movements stiff. "Damn it, you need your medicine. You might end up worse off than ever. We've got to get you—"

"Stop it, Kyle," Daniel said, the words low and sad.

A shudder shook Kyle, then he slumped into an armchair. "Oh, God," he muttered hoarsely. "Oh, my God."

"Tell me," Daniel said.

"You're so *god-awful perfect*, Dan." The emotion in his voice verged on hysteria. "What do you know about reality? You took the brass ring. And what did

I get? Italy. The whole damn thing went wrong, right
from the start. You have no idea...you can't begin to
imagine what it was like. As soon as I got to Rome the
problems started. Phil-Ital was filled with incompe-
tents and naive fools." He ran a shaking hand over his
face. "If they... if they didn't screw up, they were
stabbing me in the back. For eight years—*eight
years*—I held it together by sheer willpower. Then
willpower wasn't enough. I know some powerful people in Italy," he said, pride entering his voice as he
glanced up. "But then even the... the other interests
I have in Europe weren't enough to keep it going. The
law was cracking down. And I knew when the Italian
government started snooping around I had to do
something." He threw Daniel a defiant look. "Damn
it, you couldn't expect me to just tamely go off to
some stinking hellhole of a prison. They lose people
in those places."

Daniel leaned against the wall, his eyes closed for a
long time. Evidently he understood the garbled explanation, for he asked no questions. Finally he
opened his eyes and looked at his brother. "Why
didn't you come to me in the beginning? I would have
helped you."

Kyle laughed shortly. "Just like you always did? So
you could look at me in that icy, patronizing way while
you cleaned up my mess? Damn it, for once I wanted
to come out on top. For once I wanted to be the win-
ner. Besides," he said, his voice sneering, "I needed
more than you could afford to give me. I needed it
all."

Daniel slowly lowered his gaze. "So you decided to rob me not only of my company, but of the rest of my life?" he asked calmly.

"No!" The word was explosive. "I never intended for you to die."

Standing beside the door, Amanda didn't say anything. But she knew he was lying. No matter what she had said to Daniel, she knew from his conversation with Ted that Kyle had been waiting for the two-year period to end.

Daniel laughed, a harsh, ugly sound. "That was kind of you, brother. You only intended for me to be a vegetable. To be locked away for the rest of my life."

"No, no," he protested. "Only for a little while, while I straightened things out. I didn't expect—"

"You didn't expect to see me alive and kicking butt," Daniel said, his smile sardonic. "Face it, Kyle. For once in your life, face what you did. There was no way out for you. If you had let them release me from Greenleigh, I would have found out what you had done to the company."

Kyle dropped his gaze to stare at his hands. It was obvious that he had given up. He didn't deny Daniel's accusation because he knew he couldn't.

Daniel began to pace before his brother like a trial lawyer giving his closing argument to the jury. "What's fair, Kyle?" he asked pleasantly. "An eye for an eye is fair, don't you think? I think if you were locked away for the rest of your life—or at least as much of it as California law allows—if you were robbed of your dignity, your freedom of choice—yes, that's fair."

"No, Dan, no," Kyle whispered desperately, staring at his brother with wide eyes. "For God's sake, man, I'm your brother."

Daniel threw back his head and laughed. For several terrible seconds it echoed through the room. Then, shaking his head, he said, "That goes both ways, you know. Fraternal devotion didn't seem to hamper you to a noticeable degree. No, Kyle, you chose to forget, and so will I."

Amanda had watched the whole thing in silence, but now she stepped forward. She couldn't let this continue. Dan's face showed anger and even hatred. What it didn't show was the pain she knew he was feeling, the deep betrayal, the shattering of the love he had once had for his brother.

If she let him carry this through, if she said nothing and he caused his brother to be put into prison, it would ruin Daniel. He would bury his emotions even deeper inside him. Danny would disappear completely, and Daniel would be the worse for it. Happiness and contentment would slide even farther from his grasp.

"Daniel," she said quietly.

He turned away from Kyle, his eyes momentarily confused as though he had forgotten she was in the room.

"You can't do it," she said, holding his gaze.

He frowned, examining her face. "Why are you worried about Kyle?" he asked sharply.

"I don't care if Kyle rots in hell," she said calmly. "I'm worried about you. You can't do this without harming yourself."

"I can damn well try," he said tightly.

She shook her head, touching his arm. "No, you can't. I'm not guessing or speculating about this; I know it as sure as I'm standing here. You'll never be able to live with yourself. You'll remember your father and you'll remember Lena, and guilt will eat you alive."

Turning away from her, he walked to the window. The silence drew out as he stared at the sky. At once he relaxed and turned back to face her. "You're right. I can't do it. Not to Kyle."

He walked to the telephone his brother had used earlier. "But I can do it to Sutherland."

As Daniel talked to the district attorney, an old friend, Amanda watched Kyle slip out of the room, unsure of whether Daniel noticed or not.

She shouldn't have wondered. When the door closed behind the younger man, Daniel slumped slightly. Replacing the phone, Daniel turned back to Amanda.

"Sean will have men here before Sutherland's crew gets here," he said, then ran a hand through his hair as he glanced around the room, almost as though he were at a loss. "I guess you'll be glad when things get back to normal," he said.

Normal, she thought, feeling strangely drained. She didn't think she would recognize normal anymore, but she nodded. "Yes, I guess so. I've . . . I've got a lot to do. Another job. An apartment. Getting my furniture out of storage." Her voice trailed away. "And you," she said. "You'll be able to get back to Philton."

He simply stared at her for a moment, then he said bluntly, "I'd like to see you again, Amanda. I've never desired a woman the way I desire you. I know at first you resented the physical attraction between us, but now you seem to have accepted it. There's no need for it to stop."

She felt the trembling begin in her stomach and spread outward as she listened to what he was saying. Desire? Physical attraction? Now that he said the words aloud she knew that it would never be enough for her. Now at the end, she knew at last what she wanted from Daniel.

She shook her head. "I don't think so, Daniel," she whispered, avoiding his eyes. "I'm not mistress material."

It was a long time before he spoke, and then his voice was slow and dull. "No, you're not."

Shoving his hands into his pockets, he turned away from her. "You don't have to stay for the rest, Amanda," he said, and now he sounded supremely casual. "It's all over now."

She felt the blood drain from her face as she stood frozen in time. She felt cut loose from her lifeline.

It was all over, she repeated silently. She knew it would come. It had been an inevitability from the time she woke to find him staring down at her that first day in the cabin. So why wasn't she better prepared for it? Why did she feel tetherless?

She glanced up to find Daniel watching her closely, as he had always watched her. She moistened her lips, raising a hand to her hair to smooth it back. "Yes, I guess it is," she murmured.

She glanced around the room in confusion, feeling that she was forgetting something vital. Something was missing.

"Well . . ." She didn't know what to say. There was nothing left to say. She glanced up at him and met the green gaze for the last time. "Goodbye, Daniel."

She had walked the length of the pool when she heard the back door open.

"Amanda."

She turned in alarm, imagining she heard panic in his voice. But he didn't hurry as he walked toward her. When he drew closer, she frowned at the expression on his face. An intense inner struggle seemed to be taking place.

"What is it?" she whispered.

"I—" He stared up at something beyond her, shoving a hand through his hair. "I just wanted to say thank you for everything you did."

She nodded, unable to respond. The silence between them drew out, then, shoving his hands in his pockets, he said, "I'll get my lawyer on the annulment. I'm sure there won't be any problem."

She forced herself to smile. "That's good." Inhaling deeply, she said, "Goodbye," and walked away.

Chapter Eighteen

Amanda pulled the convertible out into the late-afternoon traffic. She liked this job, she thought as she swerved to avoid a lane hopper. Being a bookkeeper for a printing company wasn't exactly an exciting job, but then Amanda didn't need excitement. Not after Greenleigh.

In the four months since Ted Sutherland's arrest, a lot had happened. Greenleigh had been sold and was now a training camp for professional wrestlers, something she was sure could only happen in California. There was still an occasional article about Ted. His arrest had been explosive. There had even been speculation that he had killed his wife by the same method he had used on the Special Ones. But since she had been cremated, no one would ever know for sure.

It would be quite a while before he even went to trial, much less to prison. His lawyers could keep him free for years before a final decision was reached. Fresh news had taken his place in the headlines. Everyone was forgetting; everyone except the ones who were involved.

Amanda wasn't a vindictive person, but she couldn't stop thinking about the ones who had died. Daniel could have been one of them.

Not a day, not an hour, went by that she didn't think of him, as she thought of him now. She kept waiting, knowing that someday the pain would go away. Someday she would stop dreaming of him, stop wondering what he was doing at that moment, stop wishing the annulment had never gone through.

She pulled into the covered parking area that belonged to her apartment building and stepped from the car. Inside the apartment, she walked to the bedroom, removing her clothes mechanically before pulling on a cotton robe.

She knew she should eat, but never seemed to have an appetite anymore. Back in the living room, she flicked on the television set, then curled up in a chair, her eyes unseeing as she stared at the box.

Turning her head toward the front door, she listened carefully. She could have sworn she heard a noise. The neighbor's cat occasionally visited, and suddenly she realized she would very much like his company tonight.

Walking to the door, she opened it, then froze.

Daniel was two steps away from her door, leaving. He turned and stared at her with those brooding green eyes.

"Hello, Amanda," he said quietly.

Just the sound of his voice made her weak. She felt her heart pounding in her breast. Her nails bit into her palms as she smiled and said, "Daniel.

"I...I didn't hear you knock," she said, hiding her trembling hands in the pocket of her robe. "I thought you were the cat."

He smiled. "I'm not."

She shook her head. "What am I thinking of? Come in and sit down," she said, waving a hand toward the couch. "Why don't I fix some coffee? I don't know about you, but for me, it's been a long day."

She could have kicked herself. She sounded like a nervous schoolgirl. By the time she returned with the coffee she felt almost certain she could get through this meeting without falling apart.

He was sitting where she had left him, his gaze traveling around the room, stopping occasionally to study a book, a painting. When she approached the couch, he stood and took the tray from her, placing it on the coffee table. Neither of them moved to pick up the coffee cups; they merely sat in silence, staring at each other.

"I—"

"Did—"

They both spoke at once, then stopped shortly to allow the other to go first.

"This is silly," Amanda said, laughing soft. went through a lot together. There's no reas should be awkward with one another."

He simply stared at her for a moment, then said, guess you heard about Sutherland?"

She nodded. "And Kyle?"

"The Italian authorities were waiting for him at the Rome airport. He's been in an Italian prison for two months," he explained, glancing down at his hands. "I'll keep trying to get him out because I owe it to Dad, but there's just not much I can do."

Amanda said nothing, but she was glad. It was right that Kyle should pay for what he tried to do. She simply hadn't wanted Daniel involved in the decision.

"How have you been?" he asked quietly, pulling her gaze back to him.

"Fine," she said, smiling. "Just fine. I've got a new job. It's nice and dull. Oh, and I saw Ginny—she was a nurse at Greenleigh. She is still pretty upset about everything, but she has Paul now. She said that Virgie and Peter—you don't remember them, I guess—are engaged." She shifted in the chair. "Let's see, I'm trying to get in touch with John J. Pike, but no one seems to know where he is."

She closed her eyes tightly. It hurt. They had nothing to talk about now. Swallowing heavily, she opened her eyes.

"And you," she said, her voice subdued. "How have you been, Daniel?"

Rising suddenly, he walked to the window that overlooked the parking lot. "Not so well."

"Are you ill?" she asked, her heart racing in panic.

ung around to face her. Her pulse began to
e crazy when she saw the hunger in his eyes as
amined her face. "I really didn't have time to tell
. . . to tell you how much I appreciate you getting
e out of that place."

She shook her head. "That's not necessary."

"But it is . . . for me." He ran a hand through his
hair. "You unraveled a ball of twine for me to follow
out of the maze. I know what you did, and I'll never
be able to repay you."

She bit her lip to keep from screaming. She didn't
want to hear this. There were things she wanted from
him, but not one was his gratitude.

After a moment she glanced up at him, then
frowned. Perspiration stood out on his forehead.
Something was troubling him deeply. Something desperate was pushing him.

"I had a dream last night," he said. "You and I
were beside a pond and you were telling me a story."
He laughed, unaware of the way she tensed. "That
sounds stupid, but in the dream it felt right. It was a
story about a little girl who stayed in a box so that
nothing frightening could get at her. But it also kept
out everything that made life worthwhile." He rubbed
his chin in what appeared a nervous gesture. "I
couldn't get it out of my mind all day. And then I
knew why. It was because I had also boxed myself
in . . . and I had boxed out everything I care about."

He stared at her for a moment. "In the dream you
told me that anytime either of us was afraid, we would
find the other and confront the dragon together. Then
I remember how you reacted when I said those words

at the cabin...you told the story to Danny, didn't you?"

She nodded shortly, blinking back her tears.

"Maybe you said it to Danny in real life, but last night you said it to me." He inhaled harshly. "I need your help now, Amanda. I need you to help me face the dragon."

"Anything," she said, her voice harsh with emotion.

He smiled, a small, sad smile. "I hope you mean that." He turned away from her and for a long time he said nothing. Then he swung around to face her. "I'm not Danny," he said abruptly.

A wave of dizziness hit her as she stared at him in silent confusion. "What—" she began hoarsely.

"I'll never be Danny." The words were tight and hard.

"Daniel, I—"

"No, let me finish," he said, shaking his head vehemently. "I know you loved Danny. And I know I can never be what you loved. Damn it, I'm no good at this. I'm dying, Amanda." She sucked in her breath. "Not of a disease. I'm dying inside a little every day without you. All I want is a chance. I want you to get to know me—me, Daniel—and give me a chance. I think we could have something. I know I'm not exactly a prize. I'm moody and sometimes I seem cold, but—" he inhaled shakily "—but when I'm with you, I'm better. I'm more. Oh, hell, I just can't say it right."

How many times had she heard the same words from him at Greenleigh? But never before had they been so painful to her. Never had there been so much anguish in his voice.

"I would take care of you," he said quietly, breaking into her thoughts. "I'm rich. You could have anything you want. I would—"

"Don't," she said roughly. "Don't talk like that. Do you think I need a bribe to love you? You're blind, Daniel. My God, can't you see what's in my eyes?" She clenched her fists. "Yes, I loved Danny. But Danny was part of you. Part, Daniel. You're the whole. You're reality. Danny was open and enthusiastic... and a child. I adored that part of you. But I love the whole."

As she watched him, a strange look came over his face, the same terror she had seen that day in his room at Greenleigh when it had taken five men to hold him down. He was afraid now just as he had been afraid then. Only now he was afraid of her. He was afraid of being hurt again.

Suddenly a great shudder shook him, and when he opened his eyes again, she knew that finally he trusted her enough to love her, enough to let her love him.

Taking two strides forward, he pulled her into his arms. She could feel him trembling as he buried his face in her neck. "God, Amanda. I love you so much, so damn much. But I didn't know how to make you love me. I was so afraid you would shut me out."

"You're crazy," she whispered, the words loving. "We're both crazy. We've wasted four months. I think I've always loved you." She framed his face with her hands, staring at him, loving every harsh line. "I just didn't know how much until you told me to leave you."

As he pulled her even closer, she wondered if he would ever remember all of what they had shared together at Greenleigh. Then she knew it didn't matter. She didn't need the past. All she needed was the intense, vulnerable man in her arms. All she needed was Daniel.

Chapter Nineteen

Amanda bent down to slip off her shoes so she could wiggle her toes in the sand. Bending wasn't such an easy thing now that she had to reach around the great pumpkin that was her stomach.

Straightening, she smiled as she placed a hand on her abdomen. Daniel's child, she told herself, her eyes dreamy.

The two years of their marriage hadn't been the elysian fields by any means, she thought, laughing aloud. Daniel would always be reluctant to share his feelings, even with her. The stronger the emotion, the more deeply he seemed to carry it. But when he did open up to her, when he came to her in the dark with secret words, it was worth any amount of waiting.

She knew without a doubt that she and this baby were the most important things in the world to him. He made her feel it every day in a thousand ways. The way his eyes changed when their hands accidentally brushed. The way his eyes sought her immediately when he entered a room. The way he reached for her in his sleep.

As she stood staring out at the ocean, she heard his footsteps in the sand and closed her eyes, savoring the anticipation.

When he drew nearer, she turned to him, then caught her breath at the look of wonder in his eyes. Joy burst wildly inside her when she heard him whisper softly, surely, "Mandy."

Silhouette Special Edition

COMING NEXT MONTH

DOUBLE JEOPARDY—Brooke Hastings
Ellie came to Raven's Island to take part in a romantic mystery-adventure game but soon found herself caught in the middle of a real romance and a real adventure where murder wasn't just a game.

SHADOWS IN THE NIGHT—Linda Turner
When Samantha was kidnapped, she knew there was little hope for her unless the handsome dark-haired smuggler risked his place in the gang and his life to help her escape.

WILDCATTER'S PROMISE—Margaret Ripy
Financially, Cade was a gambler, but emotionally he was afraid to risk anything. Kate had to convince him to take that one extra step and fill the void in their lives.

JUST A KISS AWAY—Natalie Bishop
At first it was a case of mistaken identities, but Gavin soon realized that Callie was the woman he should have been searching for all along.

OUT OF A DREAM—Diana Stuart
Tara and Brian were both trying to escape, and their chance encounter on Cape Cod was perfect, the stuff out of fantasies. But could the romance last when real life intruded? They had to find out.

WHIMS OF FATE—Ruth Langan
Kirsten couldn't forget the mysterious stranger who had stolen a kiss. . . . He was prince of the country and heir to the throne, and Cinderella is only a fairy tale. Isn't it?

AVAILABLE NOW:

A WALK IN PARADISE
Ada Steward

EVERY MOMENT COUNTS
Martha Hix

A WILL AND A WAY
Nora Roberts

A SPECIAL MAN
Billie Green

ROSES AND REGRETS
Bay Matthews

LEGACY OF THE WOLF
Sonja Massie

ATTRACTIVE, SPACE SAVING BOOK RACK

Display your most prized novels on this handsome and sturdy book rack. The hand-rubbed walnut finish will blend into your library decor with quiet elegance, providing a practical organizer for your favorite hard-or soft-covered books.

Only $9.95

Approximately 16" x 8" when assembled

Assembles in seconds!

To order, rush your name, address and zip code, along with a check or money order for $10.70 ($9.95 plus 75¢ postage and handling) (New York residents add appropriate sales tax), payable to *Silhouette Reader Service* to:

In the U.S.

Silhouette Reader Service
Book Rack Offer
901 Fuhrmann Blvd.
P.O. Box 1325
Buffalo, NY 14269-1325

Offer not available in Canada.

BKR-2

Take 4 Silhouette Intimate Moments novels
FREE

Then preview 4 brand new Silhouette Intimate Moments® novels —delivered to your door every month—for 15 days as soon as they are published. When you decide to keep them, you pay just $2.25 each ($2.50 each, in Canada), *with no shipping, handling, or other charges of any kind!*

Silhouette Intimate Moments novels are not for everyone. They were created to give you a more detailed, more exciting reading experience, filled with romantic fantasy, intense sensuality, and stirring passion.

The first 4 Silhouette Intimate Moments novels are absolutely FREE and without obligation, yours to keep. You can cancel at any time.

You'll also receive a FREE subscription to the Silhouette Books Newsletter as long as you remain a member. Each issue is filled with news on upcoming titles, interviews with your favorite authors, even their favorite recipes.

To get your 4 FREE books, fill out and mail the coupon today!

❦ *Silhouette Intimate Moments*®

Silhouette Books, 120 Brighton Rd., P.O. Box 5084, Clifton, NJ 07015-5084
